X ₤

17266
₤

Keep Your Eye on the Man with One Eye . . .

Longarm barely had time to work up a sweat before three riders broke out of the aspen on the hillside to the south and rode into the yard like they owned the place.

"What the hell?" one of them blurted when Longarm stepped out from behind the cabin, Jean's twelve-gauge in his hands. "We thought . . . That is, we saw . . ."

"You thought the place was empty 'cause you saw the family leave outa here, is that it?" Longarm shot back at them.

The three were an unsavory lot, roughly dressed and well armed. The man in the lead had a scar where his left eye used to be. He half turned his horse so his right side—and one good eye—were presented to Longarm.

He leaned forward in his saddle, peering closely at Longarm. Then he grinned. "Shit," he said. "I thought you was dead, mister."

Longarm's breathing quickened along with his interest. "You know who I am?"

"O' course I do, you son of a bitch."

And the man with one eye grabbed for his revolver . . .

D0965177

→•← TABOR EVANS →•←

LONGARM

IN THE DARK

J

JOVE BOOKS, NEW YORK

THE BERKLEY PUBLISHING GROUP
Published by the Penguin Group
Penguin Group (USA) Inc.
375 Hudson Street, New York, New York 10014, USA

USA I Canada I UK I Ireland I Australia I New Zealand I India I South Africa I China

Penguin Books Ltd., Registered Offices: 80 Strand, London WC2R 0RL, England
For more information about the Penguin Group, visit penguin.com.

LONGARM IN THE DARK

A Jove Book / published by arrangement with the author

Jove Books are published by The Berkley Publishing Group.
JOVE® is a registered trademark of Penguin Group (USA) Inc.
The "J" design is a trademark of Penguin Group (USA) Inc.

For information, address: The Berkley Publishing Group,
a division of Penguin Group (USA) Inc.,
375 Hudson Street, New York, New York 10014.

ISBN: 978-0-515-15308-8

PUBLISHING HISTORY
Jove mass-market edition / May 2013

PRINTED IN THE UNITED STATES OF AMERICA

10 9 8 7 6 5 4 3 2 1

Cover illustration by Milo Sinovcic.

Chapter 1

"Mister. Wake up, mister, please."

Custis Long tried to blink, tried to open his eyes. They remained stubbornly closed, stuck firm with mucous and tears. He tried to move his hand, and had to try a second time before he could force the uncooperative member to rise. Then he rubbed at his eyes. Rubbed again. Was able finally to see a little.

His vision was blurred and watery, but at least he could see.

There was a little boy bent over him and another child a little smaller standing close by.

He himself was . . . lying down? Yes. In the dirt of . . . It was a path, he thought. He seemed to be lying full-length in the ruts of a mountain road, steep hillsides on either side of it. He did not recognize anything in view.

Long's head throbbed. His mouth was dry and had an unpleasant flavor to it.

He struggled into a sitting position. The change made his head feel like it was spinning, and he became nauseous.

He rubbed his eyes some more, and his vision began to clear.

The little boys, both barefoot and dressed in bib overalls, jumped back away from him, their eyes wide with sudden fear.

"Ah . . . I . . . ah." His tongue refused to work properly, so he tried again. "I . . . uh. . . ." It was no use. He just was not . . . He blinked and shook his head with anger and frustration. Stubbornly, he tried again. "Wha, where . . . I . . . Where is . . ." It was just too much to handle at the moment. He shook his head again. That motion set the hammers inside his head to pounding again.

He felt somehow detached from the world. A veil of gauze filmed his eyes.

He swallowed. Licked dry lips. Tried again to speak. "Who . . . Where . . . ?"

He rolled onto his knees and levered himself into a standing position. He was shaky but upright, and he felt better about that.

His head was still throbbing, but his vision began to clear.

Long looked down at himself and tried to understand what he saw there.

He was wearing decent clothing. He understood that. Brown corduroy trousers and black, calf-high boots. A brown-and-white checked shirt buttoned to the throat. Brown tweed coat. He thought he could feel some sort of tie or cravat at his throat but was afraid if he moved too swiftly to reach up and touch it he would lose his balance and fall down again.

He was . . . In addition to the belt that kept his trousers in place he was wearing a black leather gun-belt around his waist. The holster, just to the left of a plain brass belt buckle, was empty.

He felt, slowly, gingerly, in his pockets. There was nothing. No money. No wallet.

No, wait! In a side coat pocket. He felt something. Like marbles.

He dug a hand into the pocket and came up with a half dozen or so squat, brass-and-lead cartridges.

Where was. . . . He looked on the ground. Knew something was missing. Whatever it was, it was not on the ground nearby.

"Where . . ." He swallowed, allowed himself a moment for his head to clear. "D'you live, uh, do you live near? I . . ." He took a step forward. Turned his head too quickly. The dizziness returned. And the blackness.

Custis Long felt himself falling.

He did nothing to break his fall. Felt nothing when he hit the ground.

Chapter 2

"I think he's coming around." The voice was thin and distant. It was definitely a man's voice, not the children. He thought he heard a woman's voice in response but could not make out what she said. Not that he tried. It all seemed unimportant.

He turned his shoulders a little to become more comfortable on the soft bed.

Bed? How had he come to be in a bed? And whose was it?

He opened his eyes. Fairly easily this time.

He was indeed lying on a bed. He could see a rough plank ceiling overhead, a wardrobe to his right and a washstand with blue bowl and matching blue pitcher to his left. Something, somewhere, smelled awfully good. Good enough to make his mouth water and his stomach rumble.

He seemed to be covered with a patchwork quilt.

It lay heavy on him. Uncomfortably so. He was too hot with it covering him so he tried to push it off.

"No, don't do that, mister. You'll start bleeding again." It was a woman who said that. A care-worn thin woman with greasy hair and gray eyes. She rushed to him, bent over him, and rearranged the quilt so that it covered him.

"Blee . . . uh." He tried again. "Bleed?"

"You were covered with blood when we found you. Well, we didn't find you. Our boys did. They came running home to tell us. We brought you here in our wagon."

"Tha . . . thank you."

The woman sniffed. "It is the Christian thing to do."

"Yes. Ma'am. Thank you."

"Wait here," she said, then rose and disappeared into another room.

Her place at his side was taken by a man. Thin, in rough clothing. Longarm had never seen the man before or the woman, presumably the man's wife.

The man smiled and said, "We're Tom and Jean Gardner, friend. We're pleased we could be of help."

Longarm struggled into a sitting position, discovering in the process that he was wearing only his balbriggans.

"Your clothes," Gardner said, apparently seeing the puzzlement in Longarm's eyes. "They were pretty bloody. Jean is washing them. I don't know if that nice tweed coat will ever be the same, but you couldn't have worn it the way it was. That's the thing with a head injury. They bleed something awful." He smiled encouragingly. "Would you like some broth? We killed a chicken. She has it simmering on the stove."

That would be what he had been smelling. "I would. Thank you."

"Don't try to stand up. I'll bring it to you."

He pulled the quilt into his lap to cover himself. Lord, that chicken broth smelled wonderful. He wondered how long it had been since he ate last.

Tom left and moments later returned with a heavy crockery mug of broth. "This will be easier for you to handle than a bowl and spoon, I think, Mr., uh . . . I don't mean to be rude, but what is your name?"

Longarm smiled. "I'm . . . uh, I am . . . Oh, God!" His face turned pale and his eyes went wide in a mixture of fear and consternation. In a very subdued voice he whispered, "I don't remember."

Chapter 3

"I don't have any money to pay you for all you've done for me. All you're still doing. I . . . I don't even have a name to give you," Longarm said. He was sitting at the Gardners' dining table, the two small boys on either side of him.

"Have we asked for any?" Tom asked.

"You folks have been kind to me," Longarm said. "I just wish. . . ." His voice trailed away into silence.

"Look, don't worry about it. You got hit on the head hard enough it should have killed you. I'm betting that hat the kids found is what saved your life."

Longarm twisted around and glanced back at the battered brown Stetson that hung on a wall peg close to the cabin's door. It surely must be his, but he could not remember ever seeing it before Todd Gardner, the younger of the two boys, came back home bearing the hat as if it were a trophy. The back of the sturdy 4X beaver was crushed, and there was blood inside the sweatband.

Longarm's clothing was outside drying on the clothesline. He had been given some of Tom's things to wear while his own things dried. He suspected he was an odd sight now. Tom Gardner was a good head shorter than he, so his wrists stuck out, as did his ankles. His boots were . . . He had no idea where his boots were, or his empty gunbelt, or much of anything else that he might once have owned. Now his only possessions were a folding pocketknife and a bandana.

He could remember nothing of his past. Not his name. Not how he came to be on that road or when. Not the person or persons who did this to him.

Yet he had the nagging idea that there was some very good reason why he was here and something he needed to do.

He just wished he knew what the hell those things were.

"Do you feel up to taking some solid food?" Jean asked.

Longarm smiled. "That sounds wonderful, thanks."

Chapter 4

"I'm not sure you are really up to this quite yet, mister," Jean Gardner said, a worried look in her eyes. 'Mister' was what the family had come to substitute for Longarm's name. Over the past few days he had come to accept it almost as if it in fact *were* his name.

"You're mighty nice," he said, "all of you, but I'm beginnin' to feel like a bum, taking your food an' not doing a thing to earn my keep."

"You don't have to do a thing," Tom said. "You are more than welcome in this house."

"An' I thank you for that, but I'd like to do something to help out. I'll go easy," he promised, "an' if I get to feeling puny, I'll set down an' rest a bit."

"All right," Tom said. "Since you insist. But don't try to do anything heavy."

"I won't," Longarm said.

"Then finish your **breakfast**. It's time to be going into the hole."

"What'll we be doin' today?" Longarm asked.

"Mucking out," **Gardner** said.

Tom's work was a **mine** adit that he was slowly, laboriously boring into a mountainside. He had a routine that he followed. Two days to drill holes in the rock face and the evening of the second to set dynamite charges in those holes and blow a new face. One day to clean out the rock that had been blasted away and trundle it outside by way of a sturdy cart. Three days to break the rock and sort out the best pieces of gold-laden ore. That went into the heavy wagon.

Then every four or five weeks, whenever the wagon was full enough, Tom drove down the mountain twenty-odd miles to a stamp mill and smelter where his ore was converted into gold, plus silver and some lesser metals.

"The way it works," he had explained, "I leave before dawn. That gets me in town before noon. I stop first at the smelter. They assign me a bin to unload my ore into. They keep it separate so they know whose ore is which. Once I unload, I go over to the office and they pay me for my last delivery. Then I shop for whatever Jean has on her list. Buy food for us and grain for the horses."

"Rolled oats," Jean put in. She laughed. "You're eating some of that horse feed now." She gestured toward the bowl of porridge Longarm had just finished.

"Once the wagon is loaded for the return trip,"

Tom said, "I stop at the bank to deposit anything left over from the shopping." He spread his hands as if to indicate there was nothing simpler. "And then it's home by evening."

"There is a town closer," Jean said, "but it is, um, not a very nice place."

"She's being charitable," Tom said. "Jensenville is a hellhole, plain and simple."

"Jensenville," Longarm repeated, thinking about the name. It meant nothing to him. He might never have heard it before. And yet it was the closest town. It seemed very likely that the person, or persons, who nearly killed him came from Jensenville.

He pushed back from the table and stood. His strength was returning, slowly but surely. He still got sudden, piercing headaches sometimes. They came on without warning and felt like they would split his head in two. He never acknowledged them aloud, although he suspected the agonizing pain was reflected on his face when they happened.

"Are you ready, Tom?"

"Are you sure you feel up to this so soon?"

"Absolutely. I need to get off my," he glanced down at the boys, who were hanging on every word the grownups spoke, "off my duff. Move around some. Get back in shape, so to speak."

"Then let's go. I have an old pair of gloves that you can use."

"Those old things?" Jean protested.

"The man has to use *some* protection on his hands, dear," Tom said.

"Yes, of course, but give him the best ones. Mister isn't used to cleaning up rock."

"Yes, dear." Gardner bent and gave his wife a quick kiss on the forehead, tousled the hair of each of his sons, and motioned to Longarm. "Come on then. If you insist, mister. Let's us get to work."

Chapter 5

By the time Jean called them in for supper that evening, Longarm's hands were blistered, his legs felt like rubber, and he was fairly sure that his back had been broken a good three hours earlier. But he felt damned good in spite of all that. He was smiling when he and Tom washed up.

Tom was smiling too when he told his wife, "You should see Mister break that rock, honey. The man is a born miner." He took his seat at the head of the family table and motioned for the boys to sit as well. "With Mister getting so much done, I think I'll have enough ore to make the trip down-mountain in another day or two."

"That's good, dear." Jean was busy distributing bowls for the stew she had cooked.

"Mind if I ask something?" Longarm said.

"Of course. Ask anything you like," Gardner told him.

"I was wondering, why is it that Jean and the boys never go with you when you take the wagon down?"

"We don't want to leave the place empty," Tom told him. "Riders come past every now and then. We haven't had any actual trouble with them. But Jensenville is a rough place, and the people there aren't to be trusted. So whenever I'm away, Jean and the shotgun stay here to keep an eye on things." He reached for the ladle in the big bowl of stew Jean had set in front of him.

"May I make a suggestion then?" Longarm asked.

"Sure."

"This time when you go, why don't you take the family with you? I can stay here an' keep an eye on things. If, uh, if you'd trust me to do that, that is."

"Dear?" Jean said, excitement creeping into her voice. "Could we? It has been ever so long since we've all been in town together. Could we?"

Tom Gardner finished filling his bowl then sat in silent thought for a moment. Finally he smiled and nodded. "I'd like that, Mister. We'd all like it, I think. Thanks for the offer."

"Are we going to the city, Ma?" Todd piped up.

"Yes, we are, dear. Now, eat your supper. We need to work on your reading after supper."

"Aw, but . . ."

"If you are going to miss a whole day of school, you need to make up for it."

"We could take our slates with us in the wagon," Todd said, obviously trying to get out of an evening of studies.

"What an excellent idea," the boy's mother said.

"But we will work on your reading tonight anyway. Just to be sure you get your studies in." She smiled and took her place at the table.

The family automatically reached out to hold hands in a circle around the table so Tom could say grace over the meal. Longarm joined them, by now well aware of the practice.

Chapter 6

Two days later Tom loaded Jean and a pair of very
excited little boys into his big ore wagon and headed
for town, the boys riding on top of the ore piled in
the back and Jean on the seat beside Tom. Longarm
was left behind to keep an eye on the place in their
absence.

The family expected to be back sometime after
dark that evening. Jean left him with her double-
barreled shotgun and enough food to last him three
days. And that would be if he did nothing but stuff
himself the whole time they were away.

"We've never had trouble," Tom reminded him
before he set his team into motion, "but Jensenville
is a rough town, and you never know what could happen. So keep your eyes open, just in case. Someone
obviously has it in for you or you wouldn't have been
beaten like you were."

"I'll be careful," Longarm assured them. "You just

relax an' enjoy yourselves. I won't let anything happen to the place while you're away."

Tom touched the brim of his hat and rolled away down the mountain, his sons chattering and laughing in the back of the wagon and Jean sitting prim and proud on the seat beside him.

Longarm watched them out of sight while he had a final cup of coffee, then he got busy cutting and splitting stove lengths for the woodpile.

He barely had time to work up a sweat before three riders broke out of the aspen on the hillside to the south and rode into the yard like they owned the place.

"What the hell?" one of them blurted when Longarm stepped out from behind the cabin, Jean's twelve-gauge in his hands. "We thought . . . That is, we saw . . ."

"You thought the place was empty 'cause you saw the family leave outa here, is that it?" Longarm shot back at them.

The three were an unsavory lot, rough dressed and well armed. The man in the lead had a scar where his left eye used to be. He half turned his horse so his right side—and one good eye—were presented toward Longarm.

He leaned forward in his saddle, peering closely at Longarm. Then he grinned. "Shit," he said. "I thought you was dead, mister."

Longarm's breathing quickened along with his interest. "You know who I am?"

"O' course I do, you son of a bitch."

And the man with one eye grabbed for his revolver.

Chapter 7

Longarm hated to do it. Genuinely hated the necessity. He wanted to talk to this man, not shoot him. Wanted to ask who the hell he was. His name if nothing else. But the one-eyed son of a bitch did not give him time for chitchat before he got down to business. The man put a halt to conversation by reaching for that pistol.

Stupidly reaching.

After all, Longarm was standing there with the twin tubes of a large-gauge shotgun in his hands. The shotgun was cocked and ready, which the one-eyed man surely could have seen if he had bothered.

Instead the dumb bastard grabbed for his Colt.

And got blown out of his saddle an instant later.

A spear of flame and smoke spat out of the right-hand barrel of the big shotgun and an ounce and a quarter of lead shot struck One-Eye in the chest, knocking the man backward flat on the rump of his horse.

Longarm had no idea what size shot was in the load, probably number five or six, but at such close range it made no difference. Birdshot or buckshot, that much lead fired that close up was more than sufficient to do the job.

By the time One-Eye rolled off his horse's butt and fell to the ground, one boot hung up in a stirrup, both of the other two had their pistols in hand too.

"You only got one shot left in that thing," the man on the left drawled menacingly. "So now, what you gonna do about the two of us?"

Longarm grinned. "I figure I can kill one of you sons o' bitches by shooting you an' beat the other to death with the butt of this here scattergun. An' if that don't work out, well, I'll at least kill the shit outa one of you." His grin got wider. "The question is, neighbor, *which* one."

He pointed the shotgun casually, almost carelessly, in the direction of the man who had spoken. The fellow's face paled and he licked lips that Longarm suspected were suddenly dry. The other man fidgeted a little in his saddle too.

"I . . . We . . . uh . . . We didn't come here for trouble. James . . . he had a hot temper. You seen it yourself. We don't want shooting trouble with you, mister."

"Do you know who I am?" Longarm asked.

"Yes, sir, we do, and we ain't gonna give you no trouble. No sir, no trouble at all."

The riders stuffed their revolvers into their holsters and slowly, very carefully, backed their horses away a good twenty feet before they whirled their mounts around and put the steel to them. The animals broke into a run as the riders got the hell out of Tom Gardner's yard.

The riderless horse of their recently departed friend bolted after them, its herd instinct taking it in a rush to catch up with the others.

Blood-soaked, dead One-Eye—they had called him James, Longarm noted—bounced along beside his frightened horse, boot hung up in the stirrup, body flopping loosely beneath the horse's belly for a good thirty yards before the boot came off and his foot slipped free of the stirrup.

Longarm watched the two men and three horses race down the road in the direction of Jensenville. When they were out of sight, he walked out to James's body and stood over it for a moment.

He knelt. Not in reverence, however. He knelt to retrieve the pistol that James had dropped and to strip the fat, .45-caliber cartridges out of James's gunbelt, transferring the shells into his own pockets and shoving the revolver into his own empty holster.

The gun was an ordinary Colt Peacemaker. It seemed to be in reasonably good condition. Longarm opened the loading gate and shucked the five live rounds and one spent casing out into his palm. He cocked the gun and tried the trigger, snapping it again and again.

The trigger pull was heavy but fairly crisp. Longarm loaded six live rounds and fired at a knot on one of the logs he had been sawing into stove-length pieces ready for splitting. The pistol fired a little low but nothing serious. And now he knew.

He punched the empties out and reloaded with five live rounds again, keeping the hammer over the empty sixth chamber as a safety precaution. Then he replaced the weapon in his holster.

The Colt, the most common six-gun in the country, was almost but not quite a good fit in his holster, he noticed. His own pistol was obviously a slightly different model firearm, but he could no more remember that than he could remember his own name.

Damn, he wished he had had a chance to talk with those three. They obviously knew him, or at least knew who he was.

And damn, he wished he could go back to working on the woodpile instead of digging a grave for this one-eyed man named James.

With a sigh, Custis Long went in search of a spade so he could get started on that grave.

Chapter 8

The family returned home well after dark that night, exhausted but happy after the holiday in town, the boys clutching horehound drops wrapped in waxed paper, Jean excited about a new hat. And Tom simply delighted that his family was so happy after their outing.

"Quiet here at home?" Tom asked, slipping Longarm a half pint of red-eye.

"Mostly," Longarm said. Which was the truth if not the whole truth. The day indeed had been mostly quiet. Except for those few minutes when the visitors showed up. "I'll tell you about it tomorrow. You folks are tired now. Go on in an' get ready for bed. I'll tend to the horses for you."

"Thanks, Mister. Oh, I have something for you here."

Longarm raised an eyebrow. Tom handed him six shiny silver dollars.

"What's this for?" Longarm asked.

"Pay. Dollar a day for the work you been doing in the mine, Mister. Lord knows you've earned it. You work hard as any man I know and harder than most. I'd like to hire you permanent if you'd be of a mind to stay on."

Longarm motioned for the man to follow. He stepped outside and began unbuckling the harness off the horse. "There's something you should know, Tom. This place is sometimes watched. I know for sure that you were seen driving away this morning. Some hard cases thought they'd slip in while the place was empty an' rob you. Maybe jump your claim. They didn't stay long enough to tell me what was on their minds."

He stripped the harness off the big cob and began leading the animal to the corral, Tom following along beside him.

"You had trouble?" Gardner asked.

"A mite," Longarm admitted. He nodded toward the woodpile. "There's a fresh grave over there."

"What? Did . . . ?"

"The thing is, Tom, those fellas knew me. They said as much, but I didn't have a chance to talk to them any." He turned the cob inside the corral and went back to work on the other horse.

"Come morning," Longarm said, "I'll be giving you folks my thanks an' heading for this Jensenville place. I want to find out who the hell I am, Tom. Gives me a funny feeling not knowing so much as my own name, an' it looks like I may be able to learn something there."

"I'm sorry you had trouble, Mister. I'll be sorry too to lose you. I know Jean and the boys will feel the same."

"You don't know what kind of man you've had under your roof, Tom," Longarm said.

Gardner smiled. "I know I've never felt safer about Jean and my boys than when you've stood beside me."

"That's kind of you, Tom, but I hope you understand."

"Oh, I do understand, Mister. If there is any chance at all for you to learn more about yourself, you have to take that chance. So come morning, Jean will pack you a poke of food, and we'll see you off. The only thing I ask is that when you do get a handle on who you are, I'd like you to come back and introduce yourself to us." He laughed. "It would be nice to put a name to you."

"Even nicer for me if I can," Longarm said. He finished taking the harness off the wheeler and handed it to Tom to sort and hang to dry while Longarm led the horse to the corral to join its companion there.

Chapter 9

While the boys were preparing for bed that evening, Longarm borrowed a tin of whale oil and a cleaning rag from Tom so he could clean the .45 he had inherited from the now dead James. He sat at the kitchen table and stripped the Colt for cleaning.

Jean gave him a worried look. "Are you expecting trouble, Mister?"

"Always," he said without conscious thought.

Immediately his brow furrowed and he shook his head. "Now, why did I say a thing like that?" He looked up at her. "I hope I'm not a danger to your boys, Jean."

Her smile was warm. "We know you better than that, Mister. Better than you seem to know yourself. Do you know what I think? I think when you do get your memory back, you will find that you like yourself. With or without a name, Mister, you are a good man."

Longarm grunted. And went back to cleaning the Colt.

He was interrupted by a lightning bolt of raw pain that ripped through his head, staggering him and momentarily immobilizing him. The pain lasted only for a moment and then was gone, leaving him shaken but otherwise unharmed. It was the aftermath of the blow to the head he had taken, he supposed, the injury that had left him in this condition in the first place.

"Are you all right?" Jean asked, worried.

Longarm smiled. "Fine," he lied. "Just fine, thanks."

In the morning he was up early. He dressed and went outside to the outhouse and the washbasin to wash up and prepare for the day, then returned to find Jean stoking her stove. She already had a pot of coffee on to heat.

"Don't you even think about leaving before I stuff some hot food in you," she said. "Bacon, fried spuds, biscuits, and my famous bacon gravy. How does that sound?"

"Add some of your famous coffee," he said, "and it'd be fit for a king."

"And you will be taking a sack of biscuits and bacon with you when you leave us, Mister. But I want you to know that you will always be welcome here. Always."

"You sound like you mean that," he said.

"Good," she responded, shaking her spatula in his direction, "because I do mean it."

"She does too," Tom said, stepping out from behind their bedroom curtain, stuffing his shirttail into his work trousers. "Come back to us anytime you care to, Mister, anytime you can."

"I'll do that, Tom, and I thank the both of you. You saved my life. Literally. Can't get much more special than that."

"Now the both of you sit down," Jean ordered. "This coffee will be ready soon."

Chapter 10

Jensenville was laid out along the bottom of a narrow gulch. There was something about the place that reminded Longarm of Deadwood. Which, oddly, he could remember with a fair amount of detail even though he still could not remember his own damn name.

Jensenville . . . Colorado? Wyoming? It only now occurred to him that he did not know what state or territory he was in. He should have thought to ask Tom. He did not want to ask in Jensenville; he would feel foolish coming up with a question like that.

But he certainly intended to ask about his own name as soon as he thought he might get an answer.

He shook his head—no pain in it at the moment, nor did the movement cause any—and walked the rest of the way along the creek where a gold strike had caused Jensenville's existence.

The first building he came to was a livery. Behind

it was a corral filled mostly with mules. He thought he recognized one of the horses as having belonged to the departed James.

On the hillside above the livery was a steam-driven sawmill, which probably accounted for the slabs of timber that seemed to be the predominant building material in the town.

On the opposite bank of the creek there was a whorehouse, easily identifiable from the half-dressed bawds who were hanging over the railing of a second-story balcony, hooting and calling to passersby in an effort to drum up business.

They were homely enough, but even so Longarm got a hard-on just from looking at them. He might have risked getting a social disease from one of them—or several—except he only had Tom's six dollars in his kick. A roll with a crib whore would probably set him back half a dollar, with one of these unattractive wenches likely twice that. He simply did not feel he could afford to get his rocks off right now.

He walked on into the business district, past half a dozen rowdy saloons before he reached anything that looked respectable. That was a mining supply house and hardware.

Beyond that were a general mercantile, a barber, a haulage and freight line, a haberdashery, and eight to ten other businesses including the two-story Sundowner Hotel.

The hotel had a porch that ran along the front of the building, complete with wicker-bottom rocking chairs and a sheltering roof overhead. It looked inviting.

On an impulse that he did not fully understand but did not question, Longarm mounted the stone steps to the hotel porch and let himself into the lobby.

The desk clerk had his feet propped up on a stool and was reading a newspaper. When Longarm came in, the man smiled and nodded and got to his feet.

When Longarm got to the hotel desk, the clerk was standing with his back to the counter, reaching for a key on one of the hooks in a board hanging on the wall.

The man turned, smiling, and said, "I haven't let anyone disturb your room, Mr. Stevens. Everything is exactly as you left it. No one has been in at all, just like you said."

STEVENS! Stevens. Longarm's brow furrowed. Stevens did not seem right to him.

And yet . . .

"Thanks." He accepted the key from the man and glanced at the tag hanging from it. Number six. He had a room here. Upstairs? Likely. "I appreciate you doin' what I asked."

"We always try to make our guests comfortable, Mr. Stevens."

Longarm touched the brim of his very battered Stetson, turned, and headed for the stairs.

Chapter 11

It was like poking through the personal effects of a complete stranger. Longarm could not escape the feeling that he was invading someone's privacy. His own!

The clothing stored in the tall, stained walnut wardrobe was half-remembered. He knew without trying them on that they would fit him perfectly.

The same was true of the battered Gladstone that was tucked inside the wardrobe. He pulled it out and set it on the neatly made bed. The bag contained a box and a . . . He opened a second box and looked . . . a box and a half of .45 cartridges. And a crumpled laundry receipt made out to a James Stevens of Denver City, Colorado. Which might or might not mean that he was in Colorado now. The receipt could simply be an old one from some other trip away from home.

Home. Where the hell was his home? And what was he doing in Jensenville?

Something to do with mining? Almost everything around here seemed to touch on mining operations in one way or another.

Surely he couldn't be a mining engineer. He did not remember a thing about the complex calculations required of an engineer.

The Gladstone also held a nearly new deck of cards and, in an envelope beneath those cards, another four of the pasteboards. Aces and eights, the dead man's hand. The pattern on the backs of the aces and eights was the same as the pattern on the complete deck that was also in the bag.

Complete? He thumbed through the deck. Yes, the deck was complete. All of its aces and all of its eights were there. So the four cards in the envelope came from a different deck. But similar.

That almost certainly had meaning. Or should have meant something to him.

He racked his brain but could come up with no memory about what that meaning might be. Or should be.

Longarm looked through the clothing in the wardrobe, but there were no papers that would identify what James Stevens had been doing here before he was accosted out there on the road where the Gardner boys found him.

He was putting the Gladstone back inside the wardrobe when another of those blinding lightning bolts of pain shot through his head, staggering him and sending him reeling onto the bed. It was either that or fall down completely.

Longarm pressed his face into the meager pillow provided by the Sundowner and cupped his hands over his ears as if that would somehow keep the shattering pain away.

The last thing he remembered before he blacked out was the sound of a burro braying on the street below. Then he knew nothing at all.

Chapter 12

Longarm woke with a headache, but this one was only annoying, not debilitating. It was almost a relief to have the drumbeat of his own heart thumping inside his head.

He carefully levered himself off the bed and onto his feet, crossed the small room to the washstand, and poured some water into the basin. He splashed the cold water on his face and felt much better. Not good. But better.

Outdoors the sun had shifted to the other side of the gulch, so now it was either afternoon . . . or he had slept around the clock. Afternoon, he decided.

Longarm reached for his pocket watch. And remembered that he did not have one. In fact he did not have a vest or a watch pocket. Apparently the habit of his hands knew more about him than he did himself. There *should* have been a vest and a watch, dammit.

With a sigh he tucked his shirttail in, slicked his hair back, and picked up his Stetson from the floor, where it had fallen earlier.

He went downstairs and asked the desk clerk, "Where's the shitter?"

The question earned him a sharp look from the clerk, who must have thought Longarm was somehow mocking him. After all, Longarm was supposed to have been a guest here for some time already. But the man shrugged and hooked a thumb toward a corridor leading into the back of the hotel. "Outside. Turn right."

"Okay, thanks." Longarm offered no explanations. He followed the direction the clerk had pointed, found a reasonably clean outhouse, and took a long, satisfying piss.

He decided against asking the clerk where a good café could be found. The man already found him to be strange enough without compounding the problem. Instead he went through an alley to the street rather than going out through the hotel lobby, turned left for no particular reason, and stopped at the first café he came to.

"Good afternoon, Mr. Stevens," the man behind the counter said to greet him. "The usual today?"

There it was again. He was known in Jensenville. But Stevens *still* did not feel right to him.

"That'll be fine," he said, sliding onto one of the stools facing the oilskin-covered counter. "My usual will be just fine."

He wondered, half-seriously, if this "usual" was something he would like. Or if it too would be a mystery to him.

Chapter 13

No mystery. His "usual" was thoroughly cooked steak and baking soda biscuits with everything, meat and biscuit alike, drowned in flour gravy. It tasted like it was—and well should be—a great favorite.

Longarm ate, dropped one of his silver dollars onto the counter, and got sixty-five cents back in change. He left a nickel tip for the cook and gave the man a tip of his hat on the way out too.

He felt better once he had eaten. His head was no longer bothering him. Well, hardly at all anyway.

He plucked a toothpick from a dish of them on his way out and wondered where he might find the riders who had been with the lately deceased James the previous day. They knew who he was. For that matter, now he knew who he was. He was James Stevens, possibly from Denver City, Colorado. Or maybe from somewhere else. That remained to be seen.

The question was, did those men know what he was doing here?

They seemed to. They knew enough about him to want him dead.

Longarm smiled. If he did not know how to find them, perhaps he could bait them into finding him.

He set off at a brisk pace toward the nearest saloon.

Chapter 14

"Afternoon, Mr. Stevens. Will you have your usual?"

Longarm nodded, mute in thought. The bartender knew him too? Knew his name and his drink. Damn but *he* wished he knew those things. Yet he hesitated to openly ask questions or to make himself vulnerable to whoever—and whyever—he had been assaulted out on the road and left there for dead.

Another jolt of pain ripped through his head, nearly buckling his knees. He clung to the front of the bar, bracing himself until the pain subsided. By then the barman was back with a shot and a beer chaser. The man also laid down a slender cheroot and a block of matches.

Longarm had not had a smoke since the Gardner boys found him and had not consciously missed smoking. Now he salivated just from looking at the dark little cigar.

He nipped the twist off the cheroot with his teeth

and spat the bit of tobacco into his palm, then dropped it into a nearby cuspidor. He used his fingernail to pry a wooden match off the block and scraped it alight on the sandpaper bottom of the block, then used that to light his cigar.

The harsh smoke almost choked him with that first puff after so long being without. Then the taste came back to him and he took the smoke deep into his lungs.

"Damn good," he said to the bartender with a nod. Longarm laid a half dollar onto the bar. The bartender pocketed the money and moved on to another customer.

Longarm picked up his shot and tasted it. It was rye whiskey. A very good rye whiskey, although how he should know that . . . There was just so damned much that he could not remember.

He drank half the rye and followed it with a swallow of the crisply refreshing beer.

Comfortable and with the alcohol gently warming his belly, Longarm turned his back to the bar and rested his elbows on it while he looked around at the few others who were drinking in the place.

It was obviously the sort of saloon where the better class gathered. The men were well dressed in suits or at the very least in vests and sleeve garters.

Three painted whores in short skirts circulated, not finding any business at this early hour but hopeful.

A nicely dressed woman emerged from a back room. She was on the upper side of middle age and looked like she once would have been a great beauty.

As it was she was still a looker, with a full figure and touches of makeup beneath coils of hair that were beginning to go gray.

She would be the madam, Longarm guessed, and quite possibly the owner of this saloon as well.

The woman walked directly to him. Stopped at his side. "We need to talk, Jimmy. Come with me, please."

He nodded. Tossed off the rest of his rye and drained the chaser. "Where're we going?"

"In my office. Come along." She turned and headed back the way she had come.

Longarm followed her into the back room, which turned out to be a very nicely appointed office with a tall, rolltop desk, several leather upholstered armchairs, and a long sofa, everything done in tasteful shades of brown and green.

The lady sat in the center of the sofa and patted the cushion at her left side.

"Sit down, Custis."

He blinked. "But . . ."

"What, dear?"

"Out there. In the bar." He hooked a thumb over his shoulder. "You called me Jimmy. James Stevens. Now . . . Custis, was it?"

The lady stood and came to stand close in front of him. "Are you all right, Custis? What is wrong?"

Confused, but his interest quickened, he told her.

Chapter 15

"All right," he said a few minutes later. "I'm a deputy United States marshal. I live in Denver, and my name is Custis Long." He sighed. "So why the hell am I in Jensenville pretending to be some guy named James Stevens?"

"I'm sorry, Custis. I don't know that. I can only tell you that when I recognized you, you asked me to keep mum about your identity and your job. That's why I called you Jimmy out there where others could overhear but used your real name once we were alone here in my office."

"An' I thank you for playin' along but . . . I got another question to ask you, and it's kind of embarrassing," he said.

The woman barked out a short, low-pitched laugh. "Custis, a woman in my profession has heard pretty much everything twice over. You go ahead and ask whatever you like. I can promise you needn't worry about embarrassment."

"Yeah, well then . . . who are you? What's your name?"

Her laughter this time was louder and longer. "Custis dear, my name is Isabelle Rackham Coyne. Belle to my closest friends. And Custis, friends do not become any closer than you and I were back in Denver. Since you got here too, for that matter."

"D'you mean . . . ?"

"I mean we were lovers then, yes, and lovers again lately."

As if by way of demonstration, Belle Coyne began unfastening the buttons that held her gown closed. She started at her throat and worked her way slowly, enticingly, down the bodice of her gown.

Custis Long's hard-on began threatening to pop the buttons off of his fly.

Chapter 16

"Damn, woman, you have one helluva body on you."

Belle laughed. "Is that supposed to be a compliment, Custis?"

"None truer, none finer," he declared. And took her into his arms.

She tasted of mint and . . . something he could not immediately identify. The bottom line was that Belle Coyne tasted just fine. Felt mighty fine too, for that matter.

The woman's tits were large and shapely. They sagged a little now but not so much as to be unattractive. Her nipples were overlarge and sat on circles of dark, wrinkled flesh. Her waist was full but her hips even more so, giving her an hourglass figure. The curly bush of hair at her crotch was wiry and solidly gray.

Longarm tasted Belle's mouth again and still

could not decide what that elusive other flavor might be.

"You feel good," he murmured into her mouth.

Belle pulled her face back an inch or two so she could say, "Wait until you feel the rest of me, Custis."

"Is that an invite?" he asked, leading her toward the brown leather sofa.

"Yes, it is, cowboy. Now, get those clothes off before I rape you."

"Promise?" he asked with a laugh.

Belle's answer was to drop to her knees in front of Longarm and begin unfastening the buttons of his fly. When she got it open, she paused in her labors to pull his cock out and peel his foreskin back. Then she ran her tongue around the bulging head, nearly driving Longarm out of his mind.

He could not remember how long it had been since he'd had a woman, but he knew it had been entirely too long. Her tongue and her mouth felt so good on him that he very nearly came.

"You'd best watch out," he said, "or you'll get a mouthful."

Belle withdrew her mouth from him enough to be able to say, "Good. If you come now, you'll last longer once we start to fuck, so go ahead. I won't mind."

She bent forward again, taking his cock into her mouth, engulfing him with her warmth. Sucking hard.

Longarm responded as the urgent release started deep in his balls and shot forcefully out the length of his shaft.

He exploded into Belle's hotly demanding throat. She stayed with him, continuing to suck until the last droplets of his come were released. Then she stood, took him by the hand, and clung to him while she draped herself onto the sofa and spread her legs.

Inside her pussy was even hotter than her mouth had been, he discovered.

Chapter 17

"I have a problem," he told Belle afterward, as they were lying spooned back to front on the narrow sofa.

"What's that, lover?" the lusty woman asked.

"I was robbed. Don't have but a couple dollars to my name. Are you sure I work for the government?"

"Yes, I already told you. You're a deputy United States marshal. Your home office is down in Denver."

"Then the government would stand you good if you was to make me a loan, wouldn't it?"

"Yes, I'm sure it would," she said.

"Then, um . . ."

Belle laughed. "How much do you think you need, Custis?"

"Damn if I know," he admitted, "since I don't know why in hell I'm here to begin with or what I'm supposed to do here."

"All right. Shall we say, oh, do you think a hundred would do?"

"More'n enough, probably."

"Fine," she said. "Consider yourself bankrolled." She crawled over him and stood, stretched, then walked naked to the big rolltop desk and opened one of the many small drawers. She brought out a sheaf of gold-back currency. Belle peeled off a pair of fifties, picked up the trousers Longarm had discarded, and shoved the bills into one of his pockets.

"That takes care of that," she said. Then she laughed again. "And if the government doesn't reimburse me, I'll still consider it a worthwhile investment just for that fuck." She winked at him. "And for any more you might decide to give me."

Longarm smiled. "You're a mighty good lady to know."

"You better believe it, cowboy." With a sigh she added, "But I suppose I should get to work now." She picked up her dress and began preparing herself to be seen in public again. While she fussed with her hair—which had become more than a little mussed while they romped minutes earlier—she said over her shoulder, "If there is anything you need . . . Jimmy . . . just tell me. I'll do whatever I can. Just don't let anyone overhear, not even my employees."

Longarm raised an eyebrow. Belle said, "This town is run pretty tightly, Custis. The boss is a man named Carter. Anton Louis Carter. Boss Carter." She sniffed. "The son of a bitch likes to be called Boss."

"Who is he and what's his hold on the town?"

"The man is a fat slob. I'm told he used to be a good man with a fast gun. Now he is just a rich, mean son of a bitch. He owns the diggings that provide

employment for ninety-five percent of the people
around here. He keeps everyone in line with a bunch
of goons who use ax handles or, if they have to, six-
guns. They aren't afraid to break a man's head, break
his spirit, or put him six feet under if he won't toe
the line. And he is cheap. The miserable piece of shit
has half the money in the world and still wants more."
Then she laughed and added, "And I have the other
half. I run most of the saloons and the girls and kick
back plenty to Boss and still I have money to burn.
God knows how much he must have. Or why he wants
so much more."

"What about the local law?"

Belle snorted. "There is a town marshal, but he is
just Boss's chief enforcer. He runs the goons for Boss
and does whatever Boss wants."

"County sheriff?"

"I assume there is an organized county, but I don't
know where the county seat is or who the sheriff
would be."

"I suppose the sheriff would name the town marshal as his deputy for this area anyway. That's the
way things usually work." He had no idea how he
knew that, but he was sure it was true.

Longarm got up and began to dress. "I wonder
why I'm here. Bein' rich ain't a crime in this country.
Even bein' a son of a bitch is legal enough."

"I can't help you with that, Custis. You never told
me why you were here, just that you want me to keep
quiet about who you really are."

He finished dressing and gave the woman a kiss.
"I owe you."

"I know how you can pay me," she said, reaching down and tweaking his dick through the cloth of his trousers.

"Ouch!"

Belle chuckled and headed for the door. "All right, dear. You're Jimmy Stevens again now."

Chapter 18

When he stepped out into the saloon, Longarm practically ran into one of the men who had been at Tom Gardner's place the day Longarm killed their companion.

"You!" Longarm blurted, his hand flashing to the butt of the single-action revolver in his holster.

This one was the one who had been so belligerent to begin with but then quickly backed away under the threat of Longarm's shotgun.

He was, Longarm quickly saw, the sort of man who made an excellent bully, cruel when he was on top but with no guts when someone stood up to him. Now, as he had that day, he very quickly backed away, tossing his hands out away from his gun and literally stepping backward several paces.

Before Longarm could ask him anything, the man spun on his heels and quick-stepped the hell out of the place.

Slightly bemused, Longarm walked over to the bar and asked the barkeep, "Any idea who that fella was?"

"You mean the customer you just drove outa here?"

Belle was two steps behind Longarm. She came up beside him and said, "If you know the man, Andy, tell Mr. Stevens who he is."

"Yes, ma'am," Andy said deferentially, bobbing his head. To Longarm he said, "His name is Chuck Wilson. Works for Boss and part-time for Marshal Mendenhall."

Longarm nodded. "Thank you."

"Andy," Belle said, "anything Jimmy wants, he gets. On the house."

"Yes, ma'am," the barkeep said. "Even, um," he inclined his head toward the back of the room, where a pair of whores were chattering, there being no business for them at this time of day.

"Yes, even if he wants to get laid. Mr. Stevens is my personal friend."

"Yes, ma'am." Andy shifted his gaze to Longarm. "Well, sir?"

"Rye whiskey. Beer chaser," Longarm said.

"Yes, sir. Our best." He turned away to fetch the drinks.

Belle touched Longarm on the elbow and said, "If there is anything else you need, Mr. Stevens, please let me know."

"Thank you very much, Miz Coyne. I expect I'll be by to see you again before too long." He dipped his chin and touched the brim of his Stetson to the lady, who then turned and whisked away toward her private—and, Longarm thought, very pleasant—office.

So, Longarm mused as he sipped the really very excellent rye, it was one of Boss Carter's goons that he killed back there at Gardner's place.

If he had been here openly, under his own name, he thought, he could have just marched in and confronted this Boss Carter person. As it was . . . he still had no idea why in hell he was here under an assumed name.

For that matter, he still had no idea why in hell he was here at all!

He had another sip of the whiskey and then a swallow of the beer.

Chapter 19

"Another?" the barman asked solicitously.

Longarm shook his head. "No, thanks, Andy." He left a nickel tip beside his empty beer mug, lifted his hat and reset it comfortably, then headed for the front door.

He was getting a little hungry, so he turned toward a café in the next block. As he stepped down off the boards of the sidewalk to cross over to the next line of storefronts, he heard a grunt and a rush of footsteps coming out of the alley on his right.

Longarm ducked his shoulder and drove into the man who was charging him.

There were two, he quickly saw. The two who had been at Gardner's, including the one who had rabbitted from the saloon minutes earlier. The son of a bitch must have hurried to get his pal, and then the pair of them lay in wait for Longarm to finish drinking.

Probably they were hoping to find him drunk and relatively helpless.

They didn't.

Longarm tucked his shoulder in and ducked underneath the swing of a lead-filled cosh that the larger man aimed at his head. While he was down there, he drove a fist upward into the man's gut, doubling him over and driving the wind out of him. Bastard had bad breath.

Longarm hooked a boot behind the fellow's left foot and half punched, half pushed him again, sending him toppling backward into the other bullyboy.

The two of them went down in a sprawl, arms and legs flying, entangling themselves all the more when they tried to scramble back onto their feet.

"Y'know, boys," Longarm said, "between ya you don't make one half-assed brawler. You both oughta take up a different line o' work."

The two managed to untangle themselves and crawl onto their feet. The smaller of the pair, the one who had fled from Longarm back there in the saloon, puffed himself up as tall as he could get and reached into a shirt pocket.

For a moment Longarm thought the man intended to bring out a knife or a derringer. Instead he produced a copper star with the single word DEPUTY engraved on it. The fellow showed it to Longarm and said, "You're under arrest."

Longarm nodded. "All right. For what?"

"For murder. You killed James Murdock. Shot him down in cold blood. Me an' Cory will stand witness. That's what you're under arrest for."

Cory was still doubled over. He started puking up whatever he might have eaten for the past three days.

"Funny way of making an arrest," Longarm drawled.

"You're a bad one. We already seen you murder one man. We didn't want to be next."

"Well you came damn close to it. Now, where is the judge? I want to see a judge right away, get this bullshit dropped. You don't neither one of you have jurisdiction outside the town."

He did not actually know that. The men could have been deputized by the county sheriff—if there was one—and not just by Boss and his tame town marshal. But it seemed a good enough gamble.

"Jur . . . juris . . . What the hell is that stuff that you say we ain't got?"

"It is the right an' the duty to enforce the law in a particular place. A town or a county or a state or whatever. I want to point out that I was miles outside this here town when you three assholes tried to rob the Gardners while they were away. An' I will stand witness to *that*," Longarm said, hooking his thumbs into his cartridge belt by way of emphasis.

"The judge is busy," the smaller one growled.

"He'll agree with us anyway," Cory said, wiping vomit from his lips with the back of his hand.

Longarm snorted derisively. "The judge belongs to Boss too, does he?"

"I don't know what you mean by that, mister."

"Why don't you two lightweights run back and tell Boss if he wants to see me, all he has to do is to ask. Now, go on. Shoo, before I get pissed off an' do something to hurt you." He waved his hand as if sweeping crumbs off the dinner table.

Both deputies stepped around Longarm, and when they reached the street, they began trotting briskly toward the east.

Longarm strolled on toward the café. He was still hungry.

Chapter 20

Longarm pushed away from the table and stood, a decent meal warming his gut. He walked over to the café's counter and pulled a five-dollar half eagle from his pocket to pay the owner. Just as he reached the counter, a bolt of pain shot out of nowhere, feeling like it would split his head in half.

The pain buckled his knees. He grabbed onto the counter to steady himself.

"Are you all right, mister?" The proprietor's voice sounded like it was coming from the far end of a very dark tunnel. The sensation lasted for only a moment, as did the breathtaking pain.

Longarm blinked and shook his head.

"I asked, are you all right?" the café owner repeated.

Longarm looked at him and sucked in a breath. He nodded. "Yeah. I'm fine. Thank you."

"You're awful pale. Do you want to set down again? You're welcome to stay awhile more."

"Thank you, but I'll be fine now. Just a . . . a quick spell there. It's gone now."

"If you say so."

Longarm paid the man for his lunch then stepped outside. He felt drained of energy.

And pissed off. He knew his name and the fact that he was a deputy marshal. But he did not remember those things. He only knew them because Belle Coyne told him about them. He still had no memory of his own, still did not know why he was here in Jensenville under the name Stevens.

He was not likely to learn anything, though, by standing here on the sidewalk. He reached for a cheroot, nipped the twist off with his teeth and spat the bit of tobacco into the street. He snapped a match aflame with his thumbnail, lighted the little cigar, and resumed his round of Jensenville's saloons.

Four saloons and five beers later he wobbled back to the hotel and up to his room. He carefully locked the door before he kicked his boots off, removed his hat and coat and gunbelt, and lay down on the lumpy bed, his head throbbing with a deep, insistent pain.

Within seconds he was sound asleep and snoring.

Chapter 21

Another of those stabbing, throbbing headaches woke him after what seemed like a very short sleep, certainly not long enough to make him feel rested or energetic. He sat up and rubbed at his eyes with the heels of both hands.

When the pain subsided, mostly anyway, he got up and dressed again. He went downstairs and asked the desk clerk, "Is there a doctor here?"

"In the hotel, you mean?"

Longarm put a damper on his impatience and said, "No, I mean is there a doctor in Jensenville?"

"Sure. You go . . ." The man gave him directions to a doctor's office above the Wild Place Saloon near the far end of town.

Longarm set off in that direction, and by the time he reached it, he felt so much better just from the vigorous exercise that he very nearly turned around and went back to the hotel.

Still, since he had come that far, he decided he might as well go the few extra steps required to see the doctor. He mounted the stairs that provided an outside entrance to Dr. Wendell Morrison's office and living quarters.

The office side of the suite was equipped with little other than a desk, a few chairs, a long table, and a cabinet with small boxes and bottles in it. Morrison himself was a younger man than Longarm might have expected. He was small and slightly built and had a straggly goatee that failed to make the man appear any older. A diploma from a medical school in Baltimore suggested he was a fully trained doctor, but to Longarm he looked like a teenager.

"What can I do for you, Mr. Stevens?" Morrison asked.

Longarm paused. "You know me? Have I been here before?" He was wondering if he had some serious problem, something that came on before he was attacked out there on the road near the Gardners'.

Morrison frowned. "You don't remember?"

Longarm sighed. That cat was out of the bag now, dammit. He helped himself to a chair beside Morrison's desk and told the young doctor the whole thing. The blows to his head. The headaches. The complete loss of memory.

"That can be serious," Morrison said. "I'm going to give you some powders. Take one first thing in the morning, again at noon, and another before going to bed at night. You mix them in water, mind. Not in whiskey or beer or anything like that. Water only. I can't emphasize that too strongly. In water."

While the man spoke, he was busy measuring out small quantities of a white powder and securing each prescribed portion in folded, wax-coated paper. When he was done, he put the half dozen papers into an envelope and handed that to Longarm.

"If these don't give you relief and you still have no memory in three days, come see me again." He smiled encouragingly. "We will find an answer to this, Mr. Stevens."

"Thank you, sir. How much will, um . . . ?"

"Two dollars, please."

Longarm paid the man and left, taking his envelope of powders with him.

Chapter 22

Whatever it was that Morrison had put into the envelopes tasted, plain and simple, like shit. Not literally of course, but it did taste terrible, sharp on the tongue and the nasty flavor remaining in his mouth as an aftertaste.

The doctor, he recalled, had said to mix the powder in water, not beer or whiskey, and had even provided a glass of water so Longarm could take the first dose of medicine. The man had not said anything about avoiding those beverages afterward. So Longarm took the nasty powder, then headed downstairs to the Wild Place.

The Wild Place Saloon was anything but wild when Longarm walked into it. A pair of men in muddy clothing, up out of the mines he assumed, were leaning on the bar, and a trio of men with eyeshades and sleeve garters, office workers perhaps, huddled over a card game toward the back of the long, narrow room that ran deep off the street front. There was no sign of any whores in the place, but it might have been a little early in the day for them to appear.

The bartender was a hairy man wearing bib overalls and sweat. He greeted Longarm with not so much a word as a grunt. Longarm guessed this was not a place where gentlemen came for the friendliness and good companionship.

"Rye whiskey, beer chaser," Longarm said.

"Ten cents," the apron mumbled.

Which explained why men would choose to drink here. It was cheap. Longarm dug into his pockets and found a dime, which quickly disappeared into a cigar box on a back shelf. Only after he had been paid did the barkeep serve Longarm's drinks.

The beer was flat, and the rye was heavily watered. No surprise.

At least the whiskey, poor though it was, took the taste of the medicine out of Longarm's mouth.

"Again?" the bartender grunted, eyeing the empty shot glass sitting beside the tepid beer.

Longarm shook his head. The other places in town might charge more for their drinks, but they delivered far better. He walked out and went in search of a proper drink and a more pleasant place to enjoy it.

An hour later he was standing at the bar of his "usual" saloon. He still did not remember the place from before that assault out on the road. But they definitely knew him here, and they served very good rye.

He took a handful of roasted peanuts out of a bowl on the bar and began cracking the shells and

munching the plump kernels within. He was interrupted by the arrival of the two bullyboy deputies.

"Stevens," Cory growled by way of greeting.

Longarm glared at him. "What do you bastards
want? Mendenhall want to see me or something?"
He scratched his belly, just above his belt buckle, his
hand close to the butt of the .45 in his holster.

Behind Albrecht his pal looked nervous.

"Not the marshal," Cory said. "Boss wants to talk
to you."

"And if I don't want to talk with him?"

"Look, Stevens, we've asked nice, haven't we? No
strong-arm stuff, just a polite request. Now, will you
please come with us so Boss can have a talk with
you?"

Longarm cracked and ate another peanut. Then
he dropped the rest of the handful of them back into
the bowl. He tossed back the remainder of his rye
and left half a beer on the bar. "All right," he said.
"Take me to this Boss person."

The three of them, Cory's pal still nervous and
Longarm somewhat on edge himself, left the saloon
and crossed a footbridge to the other side of the
stream that divided the gulch where Jensenville was
built.

Chapter 23

Belle Coyne had said that Boss Carter was, in her words, a fat slob. She just had not said how *big* a fat slob. The man stood probably six inches taller than Longarm, and Longarm was well above six feet himself.

He had no clear idea of how much the man must weigh, but he would guess it at something north of four hundred pounds. Probably well above that amount. Belle had also said the man was once a fast gun, so there must have been a time when he was in better physical shape than now. He must have been formidable then. Now . . . not. Now, however, Boss Carter was formidable in a very different way. Now he was indisputably the boss of Jensenville. The king of his little domain.

Longarm entered the king's throne room or what passed for one. It was a ground-floor room, probably because Carter was too fat to comfortably climb a flight of stairs. Like the man, it was huge.

Boss Carter sat on an overstuffed chair behind an acre—or so it appeared—of highly polished desk. Both had to have been custom-made for him.

The boss of Jensenville was balding but made up for that with muttonchop whiskers that covered his jowls. He wore a boiled shirt with a celluloid collar and a string tie, a gold brocade vest, and a ring containing what was either the largest diamond Longarm ever saw or a very gaudy fake.

The most impressive feature of the big, lavishly furnished room, however, was the girl who stood beside Carter's shoulder.

She was a stunningly beautiful mulatto with skin the color and the texture of milk chocolate. She had patrician features with high cheekbones, a long elegant neck, and large, exceptionally bright brown eyes. She was wearing a silk gown or robe in the same shade of gold as Carter's vest. Her hand rested lightly on his shoulder.

Despite that display of closeness, Carter acted like she was just another piece of furniture. The big man took his time about looking Longarm over from head to toe, yawned, and held his hand up. The girl plucked a cigar off a side table, carefully trimmed the twist from it, lighted it for Carter, and presented the already lighted panatela to him. He accepted it without once bothering to so much as glance in her direction.

Only when his head was wreathed in aromatic cigar smoke did Boss deign to acknowledge Longarm's presence. He cleared his throat and in a surprisingly high-pitched voice said, "I could have had you killed. Consider yourself lucky that I didn't."

"All right," Longarm said.

Carter nodded to his right, and the girl bent, pulled open a desk drawer, and picked up a blued steel revolver.

Carter nodded a second time, and his lovely attendant came around to the front of the desk and handed the revolver to Longarm. It was his own, as familiar in his hand as any of his fingers. It felt light, however, and he was sure the cartridges had been removed.

The girl smelled of soap and lilac water, but beneath those artificial scents she gave off her own musky aroma. When she returned to Boss's side, her movement was as fluid as that of a puma.

Longarm took the single-action .45 he had been carrying and gave it to the girl, exchanging it for the one that had been taken from him when he was beaten and left lying in the dirt miles outside of Jensenville.

"You will do business here on my terms, Stevens, or you will not do business at all," Boss said, "and that is if I choose to let you live. Do you understand me?"

"Oh, I think I do now," Longarm said. It was a true enough statement. What Longarm understood was that Boss Carter was an asshole who took himself very seriously.

Longarm just wished he could remember what sort of business it was that Carter thought Stevens was here to conduct.

More importantly, he wished he could remember what business it was that really brought a deputy United States marshal into Carter's domain.

"If I do decide to let you do your business here," Carter said, "it will be under certain conditions." He paused to puff on his cigar. By then he had built an ash on it. He held it out to the side and tapped the ash off. The girl reached forward and caught the ash in the palm of her hand.

"I get half," the big man said.

"Half?" Longarm repeated.

"Half," Carter affirmed. "And if you try to cheat me, there won't be another warning. Next time my boys won't stop short of killing you." He bared his teeth in what was probably supposed to be a smile. "I hear they would like very much if I gave them permission to kill you, Stevens. For some reason they have taken a powerful dislike to you."

"I can't imagine why," Longarm said with a tight-lipped smile of his own. He paused for a moment, then said, "Half is fine. But of my profit, not from the gross. Otherwise I have no profit at all and there is no point in me trying to do business here."

"I didn't ask you here to negotiate," Carter said.

Longarm shrugged. "I'm just telling you how it is. You did say you want an honest accounting. I have no problem with that. But I have to make something on the deal too."

"All right. Half of the net, not the gross." Boss Carter frowned. "I'm wondering about you, Stevens."

"What is there to wonder? I'm just an ordinary sort."

"No, you aren't." Carter took another pull on the cigar. "For one thing you aren't afraid of me. And that worries me. Perhaps I should have you killed after all."

Longarm did not respond to the threat. He just stood there. It worried him a little that his Colt very likely had been unloaded before it was returned to him. On the other hand, men who make that sort of threat generally have no intention of carrying it out. At least not immediately.

Carter surrounded himself with a halo of cigar smoke and from within it said, "See that I don't have reason to regret allowing you to do business here. You may go now."

The son of a bitch really did have delusions of grandeur, Longarm thought.

But that Negro girl beside him was magnificent.

"Delilah, see Mr. Stevens out," Carter ordered, turning his attention away from Longarm and bending to an accounting ledger that he brought out of the desk.

Chapter 24

"Delilah, huh? You're a beautiful girl, Delilah. I'd admire to get to know you better." If he cozied up to the girl, he might learn more about Boss. And about his reason for being in Jensenville. But Delilah did not take the bait. She ignored him as completely as if he were a wooden Indian and merely led him to the door and saw him out onto the street.

He crossed back over to the business side of the creek and found a café. He was not hungry, but he wanted a place where he could sit and do some thinking.

"Coffee, please," he said to the young waiter who came to take his order. Ten minutes later he was smiling when he laid a dime down to cover the cost of the coffee plus a nice tip for the kid.

He went back out onto the board sidewalk and turned toward the saloon at the end of the street.

"Is Belle here?" he asked the barkeep.

The man inclined his head toward the back. "Thanks."

He tapped lightly on the door and heard an answering "Come."

"I was kinda hoping to," he said by way of greeting, after he stepped inside Belle's private office suite.

"You're confusing me, Custis. You were hoping to what?"

"Come," he said, grinning.

Belle laughed and came to him, lifting her face for a welcoming kiss. Which he was pleased to deliver. The woman did taste good. Felt good in his arms too.

"Are you here because you're horny?" she asked a moment later.

"I am. But that's not why I'm here."

"Then why?"

Longarm said, "I got to thinking. You said something before about not giving me away, I mean about going along with me being James Stevens and about my job. Well, um, d'you know what my job is? The pretend one, I mean, not about bein' a deputy."

"Yes, I know what your pretend job is, Custis. Jim Stevens sells mining equipment. Hammers, drills, dynamite, things like that."

Longarm scowled. "I wonder what the hell that has to do with anything."

"Boss owns all the diggings in the gulch," Belle said, "if that is helpful."

"Boss seems to own pretty much everything around here."

"Even the people here," Belle said.

"Huh? How's that?" he asked.

"The different mines are owned by different men, but Boss controls them somehow. I don't know how. The workers I do know about. They are given one evening a week when they can come into town and have a blowout. They get a little cash then, cash that winds up in my hands."

"You own all the saloons then?"

"All but the Wild Place, and it's a dump."

"And you give most of your profits to Boss?"

Belle nodded. "Half. About his workers, though, I happen to know . . . don't ask me how; it would be embarrassing . . . I happen to know that he pays his workers a lot, at least on the books. And oh, does he keep the books on them. He pays them well in theory, but he charges them for their beds, for their meals, their tools, and everything, right down to their haircuts. He makes sure the men have to pay out even more than they earn, and Marshal Mendenhall makes sure they can't leave Jensenville still owing Boss. That isn't called slavery, but it amounts to the same thing."

"I wonder," Longarm said, "if that's the reason I'm here. Slavery is against federal law, never mind what local law might allow."

"I wouldn't know about things like that," Belle said. "I just know about things like this," she added with a kittenish smile as she reached for his crotch.

Chapter 25

Longarm shot the bolt closed on the door and took Belle by the hand. He led her over to the big sofa. And down onto it. He pressed his lips onto hers, and their tongues fenced inside the heat of their mouths.

His cock was rock-hard and insisting, so he let it out to play. Belle took it into her fist. She squeezed it and peeled the foreskin back, squeezed it again. And again.

"Aren't you s'posed to be strokin' that thing?" he asked playfully, "'stead o' just grabbing at it."

"Oh, hush up. I know what I'm doing," she said.

"You think you know it better'n me?"

"Of course I do," Belle said haughtily. "I suspect I've fucked more men than you have."

Longarm laughed. "You got me there, darlin'." He started unfastening the legion of buttons that held her dress together. By the time he got them all undone, he might have been willing to concede that

Belle Coyne did in fact know a thing or two about getting a man worked up.

He popped her right tit out into the open and sucked on the exposed nipple, sending shivers of delight through Belle. She lay there for several minutes, keeping her grip on his cock while she enjoyed the sensations he was giving her. After a moment Belle let go of him and wriggled down until she could take his cock into her mouth.

She sucked on him hard, and this time he understood that she deliberately wanted to take the edge off so he would last longer once he was inside her. Longarm lay back and let the delightfully experienced woman pull the cum out of him. Big as he was, Belle was able to take nearly his entire length into her mouth. He could feel the head of his cock push its way past the constricting cartilage at the back of her mouth and on into her throat.

She gagged only a little but kept up an insistent pressure until he was all the way into her.

"Tight," he muttered aloud.

Belle mumbled something in reply, but he could not understand what she was trying to say.

"Good too."

Again the woman responded, her voice muffled by his dick in her mouth. Then she began to laugh, her head bobbing and tears streaming. Longarm pulled out of her and asked, "What's so funny?"

"You. Me. Us. Lying here like this with our clothes still on and fooling around like a pair of children just learning how to diddle each other but scared lest a grown-up see."

"I know how we can take care o' that," Longarm said. He got up from the sofa and quickly stripped his clothes off. Even so, Belle was naked before he was.

"By damn," he said, "you are one fine-lookin' woman."

She held her hands, palm upward, beneath her breasts and pushed them up for him to admire. "Like it?"

"Love it," he responded.

"Show me."

Longarm sucked first one nipple and then the other, moving back and forth between them until Belle lay down on the sofa and opened herself to him, one leg braced on the top of the sofa back, the other foot planted on the floor. Her pussy gaped wide open, wet and pink and inviting.

Longarm did not have to be asked twice. He lowered himself into the heat of her body.

Belle gasped when he filled her.

"Did I hurt you?"

"No," she said. "I love it."

Longarm nuzzled the side of her neck and began to stroke in and out, gently at first. Slowly. And then faster and faster, until their bellies slapped wetly together.

He was able to hold back until he felt Belle's cunt contract hard around his cock. Then he sped up the rhythm of his strokes until he was pounding her body with his.

He felt the sweet rise of his juices flowing out of his balls, shooting up the length of his shaft and into the depths of Belle's body.

She cried out as a powerful climax ripped through her body, and in the throes of passion she dug her fingernails into Longarm's back.

He finished then, allowing himself to completely give in to the moment. The hot jism spurted out of his body and into hers as he battered her with one final, convulsive thrust.

Then, limp and exhausted, he let his weight down onto Belle. She wrapped her arms tight around him and pressed her face into his shoulder.

"Nice," she whispered.

"Nice," he agreed, smiling.

"Want to do it again?"

"Yeah," he answered. "But let me rest up an' get my breath back first."

"Go ahead and light one of your stinking cigars if you like, while I go fetch us a couple beers to cool off with," Belle said. She crawled out from beneath him and began to pull her clothes on.

Chapter 26

Longarm dipped his mustache into the suds on the beer Belle had brought. The beer was cool and crisp and easy on the tongue. "Good," he said. "Thanks."

"My pleasure," Belle said, taking a drink of her own beer. She sat beside him, her free hand resting lightly on Longarm's thigh. "Can I ask you something?"

"Ask? Sure. Ask anything you like." He grinned. "I'll either tell you the God's honest truth or an entirely plausible lie."

She slapped his leg and made a face. "Get serious."

"If I have to."

"I wanted to know if you . . . I suppose you would say, are you making any progress?"

He raised an eyebrow in inquiry.

"I mean has your memory come back?" Belle said.

"Do you even know why Jim Stevens is here in Jensenville?"

Longarm shook his head. "I wish to hell I could tell you, but I still don't know a damn thing."

"Lord knows there are enough reasons why a lawman might be interested in this town," Belle said.

"Starting with Boss Carter, I'm sure," Longarm said. "But what federal crimes would he be involved in to the point of bringing one of us deputies in? An' that bein' so, why would I be here under the name Stevens? Neither one of those makes sense to me." He finished his beer and fumbled in his pockets for a cheroot. He nipped the twist off and Belle struck a match to light the little cigar for him. "Thanks." He drew a welcome drag of mild smoke into his lungs then exhaled, making smoke rings that hung in the air above their heads before slowly dissipating.

"Do you need any more money?" she asked.

Longarm shook his head. "No, I'm fine, thanks."

"If you do need anything . . . and I don't mean just money, Custis . . . if you need anything at all, just let me know. I'll help if I can."

He smiled and shrugged his shoulders. "I just might need somethin'. The problem is, I don't know what it is I need your help with." He laughed and took another drag on the cheroot.

Belle took his wrist and drew the cheroot over to her full lips so she could take a puff. "Do you want another beer?"

Longarm shook his head. "Not right now. Maybe later."

"Any time," she assured him. "For that or . . . anything else."

He leaned over and kissed her, then smiled. "You taste good, lady." It was true enough. "Fuck good too."

Belle laughed. "Now, there's an endorsement I can hang on the wall." She patted his arm. "Go on now. Do whatever it is that you deputies do to earn your keep."

Longarm stood. Stretched. Kissed Belle again. "Thanks again." He gave her right tit a playful squeeze, then went out into the bar, crowded now as workmen from the mines began to pile in for an evening of whatever relief they could find after the long hours underground.

Chapter 27

There were only five tables in Bender's Grill. Custis Long was occupying one of them, a plate of pork chops and fried potatoes in front of him. He had a mouthful of overcooked pork in his jaws when a gent in sleeve garters and string tie slid onto the chair opposite Longarm's.

Longarm cast a baleful eye toward this intrusion on his peace. In a low voice intended to go no farther than to Longarm's ears the newcomer said, "I haven't seen you for a spell. I was beginning to think you'd changed your mind."

Lost it perhaps, Longarm thought. But changed it? From what? What he said, however, was, "No changes."

"Did you talk to your people? Can you get the money?" the man asked. He licked his lips nervously and looked furtively around.

"Calm down," Longarm told him. "You keep

squinting and looking around like that, you make yourself look guilty of somethin'."

"Sorry. Sorry."

"It's all right, just relax. Have yourself a cuppa coffee. Have some supper."

"Oh, I can't eat. My woman is waiting supper at home. But I thought . . . I saw you come in here. I had to see you. Make sure everything is all right."

Longarm nodded. "Everything's just fine." He reached for a hard roll, broke it open, and began buttering it.

"Good. That's, uh, that's good." The gent's Adam's apple bobbed, and again he looked behind him over one shoulder, then over the other.

"Coffee then?" Longarm offered. He needed to talk with this fellow. He needed to find out what the hell the man was talking about.

"No, I . . . I got to go." The balding, rather scrawny man got up from the table with movements as rapid and as jerky as those of a squirrel on a pine branch. "I'll talk to you tomorrow maybe. Around back. After I sort the mail. All right?"

Longarm nodded.

"Right. Tomorrow." And the man was gone, scuttling out onto the street and turning to his right.

After the mail was sorted, the fellow had said. So he was a postal clerk. Longarm sighed. *Probably* a postal clerk. Not necessarily one. But if he was, did Longarm's presence in Jensenville have something to do with the post office then, instead of with Boss Carter?

Damn, but he wished that he knew.

Chapter 28

Longarm sat on the porch at the front of the hotel, smoking one of his cheroots, legs extended and boots crossed at the ankle, about as relaxed as he could remember being in some time.

He was there when a Wallace, Carlton and Co. stagecoach rolled in. The coach held only three passengers. It also carried a canvas mail pouch. Longarm saw his "friend" from the previous evening come out of the Jensenville post office to collect the pouch and carry it inside.

After the mail was sorted, the gent had said. He would be able to take a break then. Which suggested that he had a supervisor to whom he had to account for his time. And that very clearly suggested that he was not the postmaster here.

Longarm was mildly surprised that a post office in a town this size could afford both a postmaster and a clerk.

He finished the cigar he was working on and flicked the butt out into the ruts of the street, then stood and ambled inside.

Longarm nodded to the man behind the hotel counter.

"Yes, Mr. Stevens, what can I do for you?"

"I was wonderin', what's the name of the fellow at the post office across the street there?"

"Oh, you mean our postmaster. That would be Herb Generest."

Longarm shook his head. "No, not him. I mean the clerk. The little fella behind the counter there."

The hotel clerk smiled. "That's Ira Small." He laughed. "The name fits, don't you think?"

"Yep. Sure does. Say, thank you." Longarm touched the brim of his Stetson and walked back outside.

He settled into the same rocking chair he had been riding for the past hour or so. He was in no hurry.

After the mail was sorted, Mr. Small had said.

Longarm tipped his hat forward and closed his eyes, rocking back and forth just a little.

Around back, Mr. Small had said. That would be in the alley behind the post office.

Longarm permitted himself a bit of a smile.

Perhaps he was finally going to get a handle on just what in hell he was doing here. And why.

Chapter 29

Around back, Small had said. That was fine by Longarm. He waited a little short of what he thought would be right—he wanted to be in that alley ahead of Small—then tossed the butt of his cheroot into the street and followed it off the hotel porch.

The alley that ran behind the post office was narrow and cluttered with cast-off trash that people had chucked there rather than go to the bother of taking it to the town dump. Longarm stepped over and around broken crates, a cracked thunder mug, and what looked to be the soggy contents of someone's cuspidor.

He came to what he thought was the post office building. An outhouse was across the alley from the back door, the alley being a good ten feet wider at that point thanks to the size of the store that fronted the next street over.

Longarm went over to the outhouse and leaned

against it, arms crossed and hat tipped forward over his eyes, to wait for Ira Small to emerge for his break.

He had been there for perhaps five minutes when someone else came tiptoeing through the alley with a sawed-off shotgun in his hands.

Longarm had seen the man before, drinking in one of the saloons—he could not remember which one—and gambling. If he remembered correctly, the fellow had a rather loud voice and a gruff manner that stopped just short of being bullying. Longarm had never spoken to him and had neither need nor desire to do so.

And now the gent was here in this alley, heavily armed and looking like he was up to something.

Longarm straightened up and moved backward a bit, not exactly hiding but not wanting to make his presence known either. The fellow with the shotgun was acting suspiciously. After all, very few game birds could be found in cluttered town alleys. A few rats, maybe. But then this man was acting more like he *was* a rat than as if he were hunting some.

The fellow looked around for a moment then set his shotgun aside and rearranged two of the broken crates, piling one on top of the other. He retrieved his shotgun and rather fastidiously spread some discarded newspapers so he could sit on them rather than on bare dirt.

He sat peering out through the slats of one of the crates, watching down the length of the alley.

Longarm noticed that both barrels of the scattergun were cocked.

This man intended to waylay and murder someone. And it had to be a killing, as no one can shoot to
wound or to disable when he is firing a sawed-off.

The question was who. And what Deputy United
States Marshal Custis Long should do about it.

Chapter 30

Undercover or not, Custis Long could not stand idly by and watch a murder take place.

He slid his .45—his own tried-and-true double-action Colt now, dammit—out of the leather and into his hand. He took a step forward and very loudly cleared his throat to call attention to himself.

Longarm was half a dozen paces distant from the man with the shotgun, standing more or less behind the fellow. The shotgunner's attention was devoted to the alley mouth Longarm had come through just minutes before.

In that direction, that is, until Longarm made himself known.

The gent's head swiveled and his shoulders swung around, bringing the shotgun with them.

"Stevens!" he bleated.

He tried to bring the shotgun to bear, the gaping

twin muzzles swinging rapidly toward Longarm and the butt rising toward the shooter's shoulder.

"Don't," Longarm warned.

The man paid no heed.

As soon as the butt stock found its place against the fellow's shoulder, he was ready to shoot.

Longarm was quicker.

The .45 roared, belching fire and smoke twice and then a third time. The man with the shotgun was driven backward against his makeshift barrier, toppling the crates with a crash that was lost in the sound of the Colt.

The fellow's fingers tightened reflexively and his shotgun bellowed, sending its load of lead pellets harmlessly skyward out of the left-hand barrel before man and shotgun alike dropped into the filth and the litter of the alley floor.

"Damn it to hell anyway," Longarm complained to the empty alley.

Empty for only a moment. Heads began appearing at the back doors of buildings up and down the length of the alley. As soon as Longarm holstered his revolver, the rest of the peekers followed the heads and emerged into full view. Ira Small and soon after him a much larger man, who Longarm assumed was the postmaster, came out of the post office into the now heavily populated alley.

Within minutes there must have been twenty people milling around in the alley, everyone pushing forward to get a good look at the bloody corpse sprawled on its back, eyes staring sightlessly toward the cobalt sky and three holes in the corpse's vest, each within a hand span of the dead man's heart.

"That's Grady Handleman," someone said.

"Is he dead?" a voice came from the back of the crowd.

"Dead as yesterday's dreams," someone else answered.

"What happened here?" Marshal Mendenhall asked as he pressed forward through the crowd.

"I shot him," Longarm said. "I don't know why, but he tried to shoot me. I shot back in self-defense."

"Any witnesses to this alleged self-defense?" Mendenhall asked.

Longarm shook his head. "No, I reckon not. It's just my word against his." He jerked a thumb toward the corpse.

"I'm a witness," a squeaky voice responded from behind a wall of gawkers.

"What? Who's that?" Mendenhall demanded.

"It's me, marshal. Ira."

"Make way. Move aside, everybody. Let the man through."

The human sea parted enough for Ira Small to squeeze through.

"I saw it, Marshal," Small said. "I was just coming out for my break. I saw Grady try to shoot this man here." He pointed toward Longarm. "Stevens only defended himself from Grady's shotgun. It was justifiable."

"You'll sign an affidavit to that effect?" Mendenhall growled.

Small nodded emphatically. "I will. I'll swear to what happened."

"All right then." The marshal turned his attention back to Longarm. "You'll need to come by my office and make a formal statement about what happened here. Why you were in this alley, for instance."

"I was here to take a piss," Longarm said, jerking his chin back toward the outhouse. "I was just finished. When I stepped outside, this fella," he indicated the dead man, "was in the alley. I dunno what he was doing here to start with, but when he seen me he cocked that shotgun an' brought it up toward me. I didn't see that I had any choice but to shoot him before he could shoot me."

Mendenhall grunted. Ira Small chimed in, "That's exactly what happened, Marshal. I was standing right over there. It's my break time, you see. I saw it just like Mr. Stevens says."

"All right then." Mendenhall raised his voice. "It's all over, folks. Everybody go back to your work. You, Johnny, and you, Peter, Amos, and Leo, I want you boys to carry Grady over to the barbershop. The back door, mind. There's no point in causing more of a commotion than we already have. Take him over there and let Doc lay him out for burying.

"You, Stevens, and you, Ira, I want you both to come over to my office and make those formal statements. Right away."

"Yes, sir," Longarm said.

"Right behind you, James," Small said.

Longarm gave Small a quick glance. The little

man was getting him out of what could have been a load of trouble.

And was lying in order to do it. Ira Small had not yet come out of the post office for his break. He was nowhere near when Grady Handleman tried to shoot Longarm. And Longarm would have sworn to *that*.

Chapter 31

"Let me buy you a drink, Mr. Small," Longarm said loudly enough for Mendenhall to overhear when both men had made out their affidavits and sworn to them at the town hall.

"I think I need one," Small confessed. "It isn't every day you see a man gunned down."

Longarm led the way to Belle's saloon and to a quiet table in the back. He saw Belle behind the bar talking with one of her bartenders. "Miss Coyne?"

"Yes, Mr. Stevens?"

"I need to speak with Mr. Small in private. D'you have a room where we could do that?" He smiled. "One that I could borrow, I mean."

"Yes, of course. You can go in my office. You know where it is, I believe. You won't be disturbed there, I can promise."

"Thank you, ma'am."

Longarm remembered that office quite well. When

he settled onto one end of the sofa, he damn near got a hard-on from remembering Belle, naked and wet, ready to be fucked. Then he looked at Ira Small on the other end of the sofa and his hard-on subsided.

"All right, Small," he said. "You and me both know that what you swore to was a lie. What gives?"

Small sighed. "I didn't see that I had any choice. Grady was dead by the time I came outside. I didn't want to see you get into trouble with Boss or the marshal. That would have put me completely out of business."

Longarm raised an eyebrow. And waited. His silence put pressure on Small to explain, and the little man did.

"Grady was my source before you got here. The complete truth is that I wanted to use you to force him to give me a better percentage. Either Grady would pay more or you would, but either way I'd end up making more on the deal."

"What was Grady paying you?"

"The cheap son of a bitch . . . I know I shouldn't speak ill of the dead, but even so . . . the cheap bastard only gave me twenty percent of face value. I wanted . . . still want . . . fifty percent."

"Fifty percent is an awful lot," Longarm said, having no idea what the hell they were talking about. "Tell me about your scheme. How d'you work it?"

"Oh, that's easy enough. Herb . . . that's our postmaster, Herb Generest . . . Herb is lazy. Bastard lays all the work off on me. Ordering stamps, keeping track of inventory, everything. So it's no trick for me to kite whole sheets of stamps. No trick to turn them into cash too. They're as good as, aren't they? Course they are. But like I said, that cheapskate Grady was only paying me twenty percent. He was getting eighty or close to it. So you can see why I was pleased to have you come along."

Longarm wished he could remember how he had broached the subject with Small, but it was very likely that this little man and his scheme to defraud the post office was the reason Longarm was here. The government tends to take a dim view of people who steal from the United States Post Office.

"Did you tell Handleman about me?" Longarm asked.

"Yes, I did," Small told him. "I wanted Grady to know that he had some competition for my business. Like I said, whichever one of you agreed to pay the most, well, I would be better off regardless of which of you that was."

"Then that must be the reason the silly son of a bitch was laying for me with that shotgun. An' getting himself killed because of it."

"Oh, my! I never thought . . ."

"That's exactly right," Longarm said. "You never thought." He frowned. "Water under the bridge now, of course. It's too late to change anything."

"Do you have cash for my next batch?" Small asked.

"Not on me. I can get it. How much do you have and how will you deliver it?"

"We haven't settled on a percentage yet," Small reminded him.

"Yes, we have," Longarm said. "There aren't any

other outlets for your stolen postage now, so there's no reason for me to pay anything more than Handleman was. It's twenty percent."

"But . . ."

"But me no buts. You take the twenty or get nothing," Longarm said, his voice harsh.

Small looked decidedly unhappy, but after a moment, his shoulders slumped, he looked away from Longarm and in a small voice said, "Twenty then."

"When?"

"Tomorrow. In the alley when I take my break. I'll have two hundred dollars' worth of stamps to deliver."

"And forty in gold back to you," Longarm said, "when you hand over the sheets of stamps."

Small nodded. "All right. Tomorrow. Same as always."

Same as always, Longarm thought. That explained how Grady Handleman knew where and when Small would be meeting with the competitor to fence those stolen stamps. He had been wondering.

Something else he wondered now was whether he should announce himself as a federal deputy tomorrow and arrest Ira Small then. Or if he should hold that back for a while.

He had no idea where Boss Carter came into the picture or why Boss was interested in him in that kickback scheme.

Whatever this James Stevens cover entailed, it must be working a charm to have both Small and Carter fall for it and try to involve Longarm—that is to say, James Stevens—in their schemes.

"Tomorrow," Longarm repeated. He stood and waited for Small to do the same, then followed the little man out into the saloon.

"Rye for me," Longarm said, leaning on the bar. There was no sign of Belle, so he assumed she was off somewhere riding herd on one of her other enterprises.

"Nothing for me," Small said. "The boss is expecting me back to work and I should be sober when I show up."

"Right then," Longarm said. "Tomorrow." He turned back to the bar and waited for the day barkeep to deliver his rye along with its beer chaser.

Chapter 32

Longarm sipped his drink slowly, savoring the taste of it. He was thinking about remaining in the saloon until Belle returned from wherever she had gone. Thinking about her body and the way she felt beneath him. Thinking about . . .

A white-hot bolt of pain shot through his head from back to front, blindingly powerful, strong enough to buckle his knees and black out his vision.

Longarm gripped the edge of the bar in an attempt to remain upright until the pain passed. He really thought he had succeeded. Until he realized that his cheek was pressed hard against the sawdust-littered floor.

He was lying on the floor, his nose mere inches from a spittoon. The brass cuspidor stank of phlegm and old cigar butts. Between that and the queasiness in his stomach from the magnitude of the pain in his head, he wanted to puke but held it back. Still, he could feel the rise of it in the back of his throat.

"Mr. Stevens. Sir. Are you all right? Sir?" The voice sounded hollow and seemed to come from very far away.

"Is he drunk?" someone asked.

"Maybe. I don't know. Not here though. He hasn't had but the one drink here and," there was a pause, "and he hasn't even finished that one. Give me a hand here, Tim."

Longarm very dimly felt himself being sat upright. Someone was nice enough to swipe a hand over his cheek to dislodge the sawdust that was clinging to him there.

"He's a friend of Miss Belle, Tim. You and John take him over to the hotel, will you? Easy now. Don't bang him around and make things worse. That's it."

Longarm felt himself floating. One benefactor had him by the shoulders, another by the feet. He knew they were outside only from of the sunlight. It hurt his eyes even through closed eyelids.

Someone was speaking. He could hear the drone of voices. Noises. None of it made any sense to him.

The pain in his head intensified. It became so bad that he wanted to cry out. He clamped his jaw closed against that impulse.

He was very dimly aware of movement. Of the voices. The sense of motion was indistinct and the voices like a buzzing inside his head. He wanted to throw up.

He felt himself being put down. He was warm now and comfortable. Longarm let go of consciousness and slipped silently away.

Chapter 33

Longarm woke up feeling . . . good, actually. Damn good. He felt better than he had since he was beaten and left for dead on the road outside of town.

Beaten. He remembered it now. Those two shit-head sons of bitches who worked for Mendenhall. Or more accurately worked for Boss Carter. The bastards told him they were teaching him a lesson. Told him he should not butt in where he did not belong.

Of course they were responding to his cover story about being a salesman for mining equipment. Meaning the current supplier was giving generous kickbacks to Boss and probably to the marshal too.

Not that those kickbacks were a federal crime. But none of the people involved had any idea that he was a deputy United States marshal. He had stumbled into their scheme virtually by accident. What he really came here about was to look into the theft of postal funds.

He had made himself available by whispering in drinking sessions and in poker games that he was a shady sort who was interested in fencing stolen property, and Ira Small rose to the bait.

The case U.S. Marshal Billy Vail had sent him about was solved. All he had to do to wrap that up was to put handcuffs onto Small's wrists and haul the stupid son of a bitch back to Denver for trial.

That, however, could wait. First Longarm wanted to figure out what Carter was up to. Whatever it was might, or might not, involve a violation of federal statutes. Before he left Jensenville, Longarm wanted to learn which.

And it wouldn't hurt if he could give a little payback for that beating.

Billy would just have to wait a bit for . . .

Son of a *bitch*! Billy Vail. Denver. His assignment here. Who he was and what he was. He remembered it all now. His memory had come back. Just like that. He was himself again. He felt so relieved he damn near could have cried.

Custis Long. Deputy United States Marshal Custis Long, Longarm to his friends, sat up on the side of the bed in his hotel room.

It was morning, so he must have slept the whole night through after being brought up here by those men from Belle's saloon.

Morning, and as far as Longarm was concerned, no matter what the weather might be today, today was going to be an absolutely beautiful day.

He was grinning when he went down in search of breakfast. Damn, but he did feel good now.

Chapter 34

Longarm walked over to the barbershop and went inside. He was one of four customers waiting for the chair, but the barber worked quickly and there were newspapers to read. Longarm settled down with a week-old copy of the *Rocky Mountain News* and caught up on things in the world around him. Before he had time to finish the newspaper, it was his turn in the barber chair.

He got a shave and a trim then went back to the hotel. "Send up a pitcher of hot water, would you, please," he said to the clerk on his way upstairs.

"Yes, sir, Mr. Stevens."

A boy showed up with the water ten minutes later. It probably should not have taken nearly that long to fetch the water, but Longarm tipped him a nickel anyway.

Longarm bolted the door, stripped, and gave himself a wash to go along with his shave. He was in the process of dressing in clean clothes when he heard a knock at the door.

He blinked. Then smiled. "Delilah, isn't it?" he asked.

"You remembered," the girl said.

Longarm's smile became wider. "How could I not remember you. You're a beautiful girl."

"Thank you." She glanced around. "Can I step inside? It wouldn't be good for me to be seen here."

"Of course." He stepped aside. Once the lovely mulatto was inside, he closed the door but did not bolt it. "What can I do for you, Delilah?" Longarm quickly swept his dirty clothes off the bed—there was not much in the way of furniture in the room—and tossed them into the wardrobe, shutting the door of that too to hide them. "Please. Sit down. I don't have anything to offer you, I'm afraid."

"No need for anything, sir."

Longarm raised an eyebrow. "Sir?" he repeated.

The girl's medium-brown complexion darkened, and he was fairly sure that she was blushing, although it was hard to tell for sure.

"Mr. Stevens, I mean."

Longarm smiled again. "That's better, thanks. Now, what is it that I can do for you?" he asked again.

"I came . . ." She hesitated, then rushed on in a torrent of words. "I came because they're planning on hurting you. Maybe killing you. You were," she blushed again, "you were nice to me. Not like most white men. Nice like you meant it and not just because I'm Boss's pet nigger. I want . . . I wouldn't want any of them to hurt you."

"Does Boss know about this and approve of it?"

"He knows. I don't think he really likes the idea, but he has to keep people in line. Chuck Wilson and Cory Albrecht are the ones that do that. I think down deep Boss is afraid of them, afraid they'll kill him sometime from behind his back." She shuddered. "Boss is rich and he's mean but I think inside he's scared. I think if Cory and the marshal want to kill you, he won't try to stop them."

"Now, isn't that interesting," Longarm mused.

"No," Delilah said quickly, "don't take it so light. I mean what I say. They might do it. I know they intend to do something. I overheard them talking. I just don't know exactly what. Or when they will do it."

"Thank you, Delilah." Impulsively he bent down and kissed her.

"Oh!" The girl stepped back, one hand flying to her mouth.

"Did you mind me doing that?" he asked. "I wouldn't ever want to offend or to hurt you."

"No, I . . . I've never been kissed by a white man. I've been fucked and I've been beaten. I've been touched and I've been whipped. But I've never been kissed before."

Longarm reached for her. "Then it's about time you were appreciated for the lovely girl you are."

Chapter 35

He sat on the bed beside her and drew the lovely girl next to him. He kissed her long and deep and soon felt Delilah respond, her tongue fencing with his within the warmth of her mouth.

The girl's lips were full and soft and mobile. She tasted good. There was something on her breath that he could not identify. Whatever it was was pleasant though.

"I never . . . I like this," she murmured to him as they lay pressed close together kissing. Delilah's arms crept around Longarm's neck, and after a few minutes her hips began to move. She ground her pelvis hard against him, and small shivers of pleasure vibrated through her slim body.

"Do you . . . ?" he began.

"Yes," she whispered. "Yes."

Longarm pulled away from her for a moment to strip away the clothes he had put on just minutes earlier. While he was engaged in that Delilah shed her clothes. She came to him naked and beautiful.

Her body was full and soft, her breasts large, brown cones tipped with near-black nipples that now were standing upright and hard. When Longarm caressed her breasts he noticed how his skin, already tanned dark, contrasted so pale against the smooth brown of her flesh.

He gently rolled her over onto her stomach so he could stroke her back and her firm, hard ass. She had whip marks that marred the perfection of her skin there.

Mistaking his intent, Delilah said in a very matter-of-fact voice, "You can fuck me in the ass if you want."

Longarm kissed her between the shoulder blades and ran his tongue up and down her spine. "Not what I had in mind," he said.

"If you're sure. But I can take it if you want."

"No. Not there." He drew her onto her back again and kissed her some more, then moved down and sucked first one nipple and then the other. He ran his tongue lower, onto her belly. Into the tightly curled, jet-black hair that filled the vee of her crotch.

"Oh. Oh my." Delilah began to writhe and quiver when his tongue found the small, hard button of her clitoris. After only a moment she shuddered and cried out with pleasure as she came.

She was wet and more than ready when Longarm moved to cover her body with his own. His dick was so hard he suspected he could have driven nails with it.

Much better to drive it into Delilah, he thought, lowering himself onto her. And into her.

Her body was hot and moist, gripping him tight as he moved deeper into her pussy.

"Yes," she hissed in his ear as he began to stroke in and back out again. "Yessss!"

Longarm's belly slapped hard against her dark flesh. Faster. Harder. Until he could feel the sweet gather of his juices somewhere deep in his balls.

His cum shot out into her, hot, gushing.

Delilah's arms tightened around him, and she tightened the grip of her pussy too, making the sensation even stronger as he shot his load inside her body.

"Jimmy, Jimmy."

For a moment Longarm could not remember why Delilah would be calling out to someone named Jimmy at a moment like that. Then he smiled, almost laughing, when he remembered that to Delilah he was a mining equipment salesman named James Stevens.

He finished inside her lovely body and kissed her as he slowly withdrew, his cock wet and pink against her brown skin and gleaming black cunt hair, now with shining droplets of cum clinging to the curls.

"You," he said, "are a delightful girl, Delilah."

She nuzzled his shoulder and said nothing, but after a few minutes she sighed and began to dress.

"Can't you stay?" he asked. "I enjoy your company."

"Me? Really?"

"Yes, you. Really."

Her smile was huge and heartfelt. "Thank you."

"We could spend the rest of the afternoon in bed, then have supper and . . ."

"Oh, no," she said quickly, placing a finger across his lips to quiet him. "Thank you. No one has ever been so nice to me and I will never forget you, Jimmy, but I have to get back before Boss gets mad at me. I just wanted . . . Be careful, Jimmy. Watch your back. Those are the kind of men who would try to shoot you in the back."

He nodded. He stood and took Delilah by the shoulders, bending down and once again tenderly kissing the pretty girl. "Thank you." He smiled. "For the warning and for a lot more. Could we do this again? Tomorrow maybe?"

"Maybe. If I can get away. I . . . I would like to."

"So would I."

Delilah came onto tiptoes, gave him a quick kiss, and turned. She peeked out into the hallway before she opened the door and slipped out.

Chapter 36

They wanted to hurt him. Maybe kill him. Certainly to drive him away from Jensenville. Worried about competition? It seemed entirely likely, Longarm thought.

He almost laughed. First there was Grady Handleman, who wanted, with Ira Small's able assistance, to preserve his lucrative fiddle of the United States government. Now it was Marshal Mendenhall and his asshole enforcers Chuck Wilson and Cory Albrecht.

Longarm had no idea what they were trying to hide, what competition they thought he would bring. Not that it really mattered. If they intended to come for him, they'd better bring a lunch because that would take some doing.

He finished dressing and went downstairs, his thoughts more on Delilah than on Mendenhall and his goons.

Longarm was halfway down the stairs when the pain ripping through his skull hit him. His knees buckled, and he clawed at the banister for support, bending over it and fighting back an impulse to puke.

He sank down onto one knee, half-draped over the banister for support.

Then he went completely blank.

"Are you all right, fella?"

Longarm did not recognize the voice. He felt a hand on his back and another on his shoulder.

"You'd best slow down, mister. I think you've had about enough to drink for one day."

Longarm became aware of a man standing over him. He himself was still on the flight of stairs in the hotel. He was down on his knees, still clinging to the banister. Obviously the good Samaritan who was bending over him assumed he was drunk.

"Yeah, uh, thanks. Thanks a lot, friend."

The gentleman stood up and nodded. "You sound better now."

"I feel better. Thanks." It was the truth. He did feel better. Not great. But better.

When he stood upright, he was still a little shaky and light-headed but nothing worse than that.

He remembered the powders the doctor had given him. They were . . . Where the hell were they? He searched through his pockets and found the wraps of paper carefully folded and put away in an inside coat pocket where he would normally carry his wallet and badge.

Longarm went back upstairs to his room. He mixed one of the powder packets in a mug of water from the pitcher on his washstand and drank the nasty stuff down. He did not feel any better afterward, but perhaps it took some time to work.

He went back out into the hall, carefully locked his door, and once again started down the stairs.

And once again his knees buckled.

But this time there was no stabbing pain in his head, no dizziness at all.

This time it felt like the staircase itself was shaking.

Earthquake? Could this be an earthquake up here in the mountains?

Longarm hurried the rest of the way down to the ground floor and joined a rush of men heading out into the street.

All up and down the main street of Jensenville people were pouring outside, many in panic.

"It's the mine," someone shouted. "There's been a cave-in."

The deep underground rumbling could no longer be felt, but the mere word 'cave-in' was more than enough cause for alarm.

People began running toward one of the mine adits where dust streamed out like smoke. Longarm joined them, racing to see if he could help.

Chapter 37

"Who's working the hoist?" Longarm shouted into the din of voices and confusion. No one answered, so he grabbed a man by the arm and put the question to him. "Mister, can you operate that thing?" He pointed to the steam-powered donkey engine beside the hoist that led somewhere into the depth of the mountain.

"No, but Hank here can handle it."

Longarm turned his attention to the burly fellow known as Hank. "You. Is the donkey powered up?"

Hank nodded. "Look at the gauge there. She has steam."

"All right. Your job now is to run that cage. An' you," he turned to the other fellow, "I want you to keep the coal coming. Keep the steam up. But not too high."

The fellow scowled. "Teach your gramma to suck eggs, mister. I been firing steam engines half my life. I know what to do and how to do it."

"Good man," Longarm said. He began circulating through the crowd. "I need a crew to go down the shaft. There's men who could be trapped down there. We need to find them and get them up. Come on now. Who's with me?"

He was nearly knocked over by the crush of onlookers who volunteered to help. Longarm grabbed a lantern off the wall, as did other men, until every lantern in the hoist shack had been taken up.

With Longarm leading the way—and wondering just where the foremen for this shift were—they boarded the freight cage that dangled over the depths of the mine shaft.

"What's the signal?" he called to Hank, who was manning the donkey.

"One tug of the bellpull for each level you want. This is level one. There's three more below ground level here. Only one horizontal adit at each level below."

Longarm nodded and held up four fingers to indicate the level he wanted. They might as well start at the bottom and work their way up, he reasoned. Hank began letting out cable, allowing the steel cage to drop into the belly of Hades.

Dust continued to billow from somewhere down there, but it was not quite as thick now. Longarm unbuttoned his shirt and pulled it up over his nose and mouth. That would make a mess of a clean shirt, but breathing clean air seemed somewhat more important to him than that little detail.

The deeper they went, the worse the air quality was. By the time they reached the lowest level, it was almost impossible to see. There was no air movement at all down there.

Perhaps, he thought, the mine was equipped with bellows that would artificially move the air, but that would require someone to operate them. Even if such devices existed, they were inoperative now, either because the cave-in had destroyed them . . . or because it destroyed the men who would normally be operating the bellows.

The cage thumped onto a pile of rubble just short of the floor at level four. The uneven surface made the cage teeter sideways so that Longarm feared the thing might become stuck inside the shaft. Time enough to worry about that later when they wanted the cage to be pulled up again. For right now . . .he unfastened the chain that was the only safety device on the open side of the cage and dropped to hands and knees to lower himself into the fourth level horizontal.

"Follow me," he shouted.

Chapter 38

The air was so foul with dust and some sort of fumes that breathing was almost an impossibility, and the light from Longarm's lantern reflected on the dust hanging in the still air, so that vision was nearly impossible as well.

He edged forward, holding the lantern in front of him but feeling ahead with his free hand as well.

The jumble of broken rock underfoot made matters just that much worse. He stumbled and cussed his way ahead, a press of other would-be rescuers moving at his back.

Longarm turned to the man at his left, the miner's features indistinguishable in the glow of yellow light from the lantern he held low at his side. "Are there side shafts?" he asked, unnecessarily raising his voice.

The man shook his head. "No. Why?"

"'Cause I don't want to get off the main line and get myself lost," Longarm said.

"You ain't been down here before?" the man responded, incredulous. "What the hell are you doing here then?"

"I'm tryin' to help, dammit," Longarm snapped. He tripped over something on the floor, cussed some more, and stumbled on, more feeling his way than seeing the path ahead.

Others pressed close around him on both sides, men rushing to help at the risk of their own lives.

Longarm felt as much as heard a dull thump ahead of them in the adit.

"Oh, Jesus!" someone behind him shouted.

A cascade of loose rock rained down from the roof, threatening to bury them all if it continued. Mercifully the tremor stopped after only a moment. Longarm felt blood running from a cut where a sharp piece of stone had fallen onto his head, the blow partially softened by his very battered Stetson.

He felt his boot encounter something soft. He knelt and held his lantern low to the floor. He saw a man's hand and wrist, both so covered in gray rock dust as to be almost unrecognizable. The rest of the miner's arm was buried in rubble that had fallen from the roof . . . and more could drop without warning.

"Here," Longarm shouted. "Someone give me a hand getting the rock moved off this man."

"Where will we put it, mister? There's no shaft to drop it into."

"Along the wall there. Pile it on . . . on that side

of the wall. Leave room enough to walk in, but pile
this loose shit off to the side there."

"Right."

Willing hands bent to the task, grabbing up the
broken rock and carrying it away, the men working
like ants as they formed themselves into two lines,
one on either side of the adit, one side picking up
rock and carrying it back toward the lift shaft, the
other side pressing forward so they could pick up
more chunks of rock and carry them away.

"Is there room for us?" a distant voice called.
Apparently the lift had been raised and another group
of rescuers lowered into the mine while Longarm and
the first bunch were busy organizing themselves.

"There will be when you help us clear this mess
away."

The man whose hand Longarm had found was
dead, his body crushed and his features almost
unrecognizable from the effects of the fallen rock.

Another body was found and, as the wall of broken stone was pushed back and the loose rock shoved
aside, a third.

A line of lanterns was placed down the center of
the adit, men moving in one direction on one side of
it and in the opposite direction on the other side. As
far as Longarm could tell, no one had ordered that
the lanterns be placed like that. The miners had simply seen a need and done what was necessary.

He joined the others, placing his lantern down and
picking up rock; shuffling back toward the vertical
shaft, placing his rock down on the side of the adit,

then crossing to the other side and feeling his way back toward the cave-in.

Gradually the dust began to settle and the air to clear. It became possible to see half a dozen feet ahead, then farther. Indistinct shapes became men, some whose dress clearly showed them to be miners but others wearing city clothes—an apron, a vest and tie. The question down here was not what a man normally did for a living or what his social status might be. Down here at level four the only thing that mattered was getting to anyone still alive in the depths of the mine.

Longarm saw a glimmer of light somewhere beyond the cone of fallen rock. "There they are, boys," he shouted. "There's someone still alive in there. I can see their lanterns. Dig, boys. Dig 'em out."

He redoubled his attack on the broken rock, picking up pieces of stone that ordinarily would have been too heavy to lift and staggering away from the pile, dropping the stone on the side and racing back for more.

Voices from the other side of the obstruction rewarded the rescuers as the trapped miners dug from their side.

"Here we are, fellas. Thank God. We're alive, we're alive."

Men anxiously asked about friends. No one seemed to know who had died, who remained.

Quickly the last of the fallen rock was hauled aside until an opening was created large enough for the trapped men to crawl through to safety. Two had to be dragged through. They were too battered by the cave-in to be able to walk on their own. Several others had broken bones, and bloody gashes, the wounds stanched by the dust, were all too common.

But the rescuers had done their work. The trapped men were relieved.

A check of the roster and the work schedule showed there were four men dead, including the shift foreman.

Longarm was exhausted by the time all the living had been brought out. His hands were bloody from the abrasive rock, and his arms and back ached from the effort he had put into carrying rock away.

But the miners were alive. Most of them. That was more than reward enough in his book.

He had been down . . . he had no idea how long. Hours. That was all he was sure of. When he finally did come up, the same pair he had assigned to the steam donkey were still at their stations, still working to provide support for the men who had gone below.

The sun had set, unnoticed, while they were down in the mine. All around him men were milling about, talking, excited. But happy.

A bunch of Belle's ladies were gathered in the light of what surely must have been a hundred lamps and lanterns. They were passing out coffee and sandwiches. And whiskey. And more than one flirtatious bawd was showing a tit as a form of advertisement for future business.

Belle herself was standing beside a whiskey keg, dipping the liquor out with a ladle and passing it out to any who wanted. Longarm got into the line for her whiskey, but she did not recognize him when he reached the front of the line and got his dipper of bracing, throat-cleansing whiskey. Either she was too busy, or he was too dust-covered and weary for her to see who it was who accepted the liquor from her.

Longarm limped back to the hotel, reminded now that he was on the surface again that there were men here who were lying in wait for him. He hoped like hell they would not come after him now. His hands were so stiff and sore that he was sure he would be slow with gun or fist, either one.

Now what he wanted, what he needed, was another bath and yet another change of clothing. The things he was wearing would never be serviceable again.

Chapter 39

"I'm sorry, Mr. Stevens. All my people have disappeared. The excitement underground, you know. Well, looking at you, your clothes I mean, I guess you do know about that all right."

"Thanks, Willard." Longarm smiled and turned away from the desk. Then he paused as it came to him. He *knew* this man. Of course he did. Willard Rush. Originally from Alabama. Some small town there. And Longarm knew him. Remembered him.

Longarm's memory was back. Completely back now, at least as far as he could tell.

He chuckled a bit. If his memory was not completely back, how the hell was he supposed to remember that it was not?

It surely did seem like it was fully back, however.

Longarm stopped and turned back to the clerk. "Willard, I just have to have me a bath even if it's only a whore's bath. Where can I get a bucket an' water. I don't mind carrying it up myself, but I got to get shut of all this rock dust."

"We have some buckets piled on the back porch, and there is a pump in the back too. I'm sorry you have to carry the water yourself, but I have no idea where my people have got to or when . . . or if . . . they will report back. I do apologize, Mr. Stevens."

"All right, Willard, thanks."

Longarm went through the narrow service hall to the back of the hotel. He found the buckets and the pump and drew two buckets full, one to wash with and the other to rinse. He expected to need that much.

There were some copper tubs there too, a pair of them, but after all the excitement and the labor down below, Longarm simply did not feel up to dragging a tub upstairs, or the water it would take to fill one.

He carried his water into the lobby, set the buckets down, and pulled out his bulbous Ingersoll watch. As he had half-expected, the big railroad-quality watch had stopped. It ran down sometime during the rescue work.

"What time is it, Willard?" he asked.

"I'm not sure. Nine-thirty or ten, sometime around then."

"All right. Thanks." It was much too late to find Ira Small and do anything about gathering the information that at some date in the future would be used to prosecute Small for theft of United States government property. Stamps, that is.

Tomorrow would just have to do. Longarm picked up his buckets of bathwater and carried them up to

his room, then unlocked his door and trudged grate-
fully inside.

He stripped off his clothes, frowning when he saw
what they looked like now. He doubted that even the
best chemical, so-called dry cleaning could ever get
them clean again.

With a sigh—he was sure Henry would never
approve the cost of a new suit of clothes on his
expense account—he dropped everything in a pile
in a corner of the room, got his washrag and dish of
lye soap, and had himself a cold water wash.

He doubted he would so much as feel the lumps
in his bed tonight.

Chapter 40

Longarm leaned over the little table and carefully wrote out on the thin paper each word as it formed in his mind.

BOSS, GOT THE GOODS ON THE POST OFFICE THIEF. WILL BRING HIM IN LATER SOMETIME. MEANWHILE I GOT MY EYE ON SOME OTHER FUNNY STUFF GOING ON UP HERE. NOT EXACTLY SURE WHAT. YET. BUT I WILL. INTEND TO STAY HERE UNTIL I KNOW WHAT THE DEAL IS.

SEND MONEY. SEND POSTAL MONEY ORDER TO JAMES STEVENS, c/o JENSEN-VILLE P.O. NEED THREE HUNDRED. MORE IF YOU WANT TO BUY ME A FEW DRINKS ON UNCLE SAM'S DIME. HA HA.

WILL SEND THIS TO YOUR HOME FOR
OBVIOUS REASONS. I AM NOT READY TO
GIVE UP BEING STEVENS QUITE YET.
   TIME TO GO TO WORK NOW, BOSS. YOU
KNOW WHERE TO REACH ME IF YOU
REALLY REALLY NEED ME.

YOUR BEST DAMN DEPUTY,
LONG

Longarm folded the piece of paper he had gotten from Willard's day replacement—his name was Curtis, and Longarm remembered that now too—and tucked it into the envelope he had also cadged from Curtis, licked the point of his pencil, and carefully lettered W. Vail on the front of the envelope along with Billy's home address. For a return address he printed J. Stevens, Sundowner Hotel, Jensenville, Colo.

Son of a bitch, he thought. Colorado. He had been uncertain what state he was in, and now he remembered. Jensenville was in Colorado. Of course it was.

He was smiling when he went downstairs.

"Got any mastic, Curtis? Anything I can use to glue this thing shut with?"

"I got a little pot of school paste. Will that do?"

"Anything that's sticky, thanks."

Curtis grinned. "I could turn that into a dirty joke, you know."

"Yeah, so could I, but let's not." Longarm took the cap off the jar of white paste and used his finger to smear it onto the flap of the envelope, then stuck the finger in his mouth. The paste tasted exactly the same as he remembered from very long ago. The flavor carried him back through those years and made him smile. If only he had known . . .

Giving the desk clerk a silent salute with the now properly sealed envelope, he headed out into the street and turned toward his usual café—yes, he remembered that now too—and inside.

"Your usual, Mr. Stevens?"

"Please." He fished a nickel out of his pocket and waved to the paperboy who was hawking copies of the *Rocky Mountain News* out on the sidewalk. The paper was only four days old. Not bad, considering.

Longarm settled down with the newspaper and a first cup of coffee while his breakfast was being prepared.

Chapter 41

The man behind the counter was balding, with fuzzy muttonchop side-whiskers and a red complexion that suggested either he had been in the sun too long . . . or spent too much time cozying up to a bottle. Longarm assumed he was the postmaster. Or simply a postal employee, although he would not have thought Jensenville large enough to require more than two men in the post office.

"One three-cent stamp, please, and do you have some glue I can use on it?" He laid a penny and a two-cent coin on the counter and collected the desired stamp.

"There's a paste pot on that shelf over there, mister. You're free to use it."

"Thanks." He used a dab of rubber cement from the little pot to affix his stamp onto the envelope going to Billy Vail and returned to the counter to hand his letter over to the gent there.

There was no sign of Ira Small, but Longarm could hear noises coming from a behind the bank of lockboxes. Small could be working there, putting up mail or otherwise doing whatever it was that postal people do.

Longarm was about half-tempted to ask to see Small, just to frighten the crap out of the little man. It would undoubtedly unnerve him for Longarm to brazenly show up here.

But after all, they did have to arrange another meeting so Small could make his sale of the stolen stamps. Stolen right out from under the postmaster's nose.

Or so the thieving mail clerk believed.

It was, in fact, the Jensenville postmaster, Longarm now remembered, whose complaint had led to Longarm being sent here to begin with. The postmaster knew much more than Small realized.

It was an error in judgment that would cost Small something on the order of five to ten years in the federal prison in Leavenworth, Kansas. And incarceration in Leavenworth was no picnic. Longarm was well familiar with the imposing prison. Inmates there did not want to come back.

He sighed as he headed back out onto the street, pondering why it was, given what he knew about prisons, that so very many crooks did revert to their old ways once they were released. It was those same ways that had resulted in their prison sentences to begin with, but many, very many, criminals found themselves repeating the behavior that had put them behind bars in the first place. Idiotic was what Longarm called it, but somehow they failed to learn.

Of course it was also true that many criminals regarded prison time as an opportunity to learn new ways to cheat and steal and con. They were an odd sort but often likeable. Longarm sometimes felt closer to the men he hunted than to straight civilians. But then, he realized with a chuckle, he spent much more time with the lowlifes than he did with ordinary folk.

He checked his watch, forgetting that he had not yet wound and properly set it. He took care of winding the Ingersoll while he walked, but finding the correct time might take some doing this far from a railroad.

Then he laughed. He suspected he knew where he could find the right time. He wheeled and headed at a brisk pace toward Boss Carter's lair.

Chapter 42

"Hey, you can't go in there."

"Stay sittin' there, fella. I can find my own way." Longarm smiled and blithely ignored the burly fellow who was guarding the lion's den. Longarm barged into Boss's huge office. Carter was leaning back in his chair. Delilah was on station beside him.

The mulatto girl was, as usual, lovely. Longarm gave her a probing look, and although he could not be sure, he thought she blushed at the meaning he put into it. For Delilah's sake, he hoped Boss did not catch the exchange.

"What the hell are you doing here, Stevens?" Carter demanded.

"I came for a chat," Longarm said calmly. "'Bout two things. First off, I'm betting you'd be about the only man in Jensenville as has the correct time, an' my pocket watch ran down. My own fault, o' course but it vexes me to not have the right time. Would you mind tellin' me what it is?"

Carter laughed. And pulled out his own watch, which appeared to be the same model of Ingersoll railroad-grade timepiece as Longarm's, but in a gold case with a hunt scene engraved on it.

"It's ten-seventeen," Carter said.

"Thanks." Longarm pulled out his own watch, pulled the stem, and twirled the hands until he got the time properly set. "That's better," he said as he once again tucked the watch into his vest pocket.

"What is your other concern?" Carter asked. "You did say you had two of them, didn't you?"

"Aye, I did indeed. The other one is, I was curious do you know that some of your boys seem to be gunning for me. I mean, I was under the impression that you an' me could do business together. Now I hear that those boys think they can waylay me, and it occurs to me that they might be running off the reservation here. If you didn't sic them on me . . . and I don't think that you did . . . who did? And why?"

Carter growled—literally growled down deep in his throat—and sat forward in his huge chair, leaning onto the desk and slamming a fist down on the polished surface.

"Are you sure about this?" he bellowed.

"It's what was told to me," Longarm said. He grinned. "As you might imagine, I wasn't let in on the planning of it."

"I can tell you one thing, Stevens. If someone in

this town has put out an order that you be killed, I want to know about it, and I want to know why."

"That's fine an' dandy, Boss, but I want you to know one thing my own self. If one of them boys come for me or try and back-shoot me, like maybe before you get hold o' them and put a stop to things, I'm not gonna stand there an' be shot down. I'll defend myself."

Carter turned his head and in a low, tightly controlled voice, said, "Delilah, get me Mendenhall. I want his ass in front of this desk inside of five minutes or you and him both will suffer."

"Yes, sir." The girl flowed swiftly, not exactly running but moving awfully fast in her elegant stride, out a back door.

Carter returned his attention to Longarm. "You've had your two questions, Stevens, and your answers to them."

Longarm nodded. "So I have." He touched the brim of his Stetson. "G'bye, Boss. For now."

He spun on his heels and headed for the doorway.

Chapter 43

Longarm was at loose ends for the time being. He probably could not talk to Ira Small again until the man took his afternoon break, and he did not want to be wandering the streets in case Mendenhall and the goons had a back-shooting in mind.

But he knew what he could do in the meantime.

Longarm lengthened his stride now that he had a purpose in mind. He strode down to the livery.

"I'd like to rent a horse an' buggy."

"Same one as before?" the liveryman asked. That was a little detail that Longarm did not recall from before he was waylaid by the now deceased James-with-One-Eye. And friends.

Proof enough, he realized, that his memory had not completely returned.

Obviously he had driven out of town on some errand he could not now remember and had been beaten and left for dead by the trio.

Now it appeared that the remaining pair wanted another bite of that apple. The difference was that now he would be expecting trouble from them. The last time there would have been no reason for him to be particularly wary.

He did wonder, though, just how those three had been able to jump him, even if he had not been expecting trouble. Perhaps the old—but often effective—ploy of 'Hey, mister, can you help us for a minute?' It would have been something like that to be sure. Whatever it was would not work a second time. Jim Stevens might not have been especially dodgy; Custis Long was.

"Dollar for four hours or dollar and a half for the rest of the day," the hostler told him while he was getting a set of harness down from pegs drilled into the barn wall.

"That's fine," Longarm said.

"In advance. And I don't want my animal coming back on his own this time neither, like he did the last time. You take care of him or you won't be renting here again."

"I'll take care," Longarm said. He meant it quite sincerely.

He stepped outside the barn and smoked a cheroot while the liveryman brought a sleek bay out of a stall, draped the harness onto it, and backed it between the poles of a light, doctor's style surrey.

Longarm paid a dollar and a half in advance and climbed onto the driving seat. He took up the lines and the whip and wheeled out into the street.

He drove down to the nearest mercantile and tied

up there. Inside he went on a spending spree. A happy one, though. He bought fancy yard goods and thread for Jean Gardner. And a hat. A frilly, rather silly-looking thing with ribbons and feathers galore. If Jean did not like it, she could give it to Tom. He could pour a little stink-um on the thing and use it as a lure to trap bobcats.

He bought two shirts and a pair of overalls for Tom.

The boys got half a ton—well, it seemed like it—of every kind of candy they had in the place, along with wooden sailboats rigged with real sailcloth sails.

He had fun doing his shopping and paid the bill happily. There was so much booty that he had to have help carrying it all out to the buggy.

"Thanks, mister. That's the biggest sale I've had all week. Maybe all this month," the proprietor said as he lifted the last sack into the back of the surrey.

Longarm climbed in, and with a nod and a tip of his hat he took up the driving lines and spanked the bay into motion.

He was smiling as he drove out of town.

Chapter 44

Longarm was halfway to the Gardners' place before it occurred to him that they might not be home. They could have gone down-mountain to sell Tom's ore to the mill, depending on how much he was able to produce on his own.

Not that Longarm particularly enjoyed swinging a pick or mucking out broken ore, but he felt he owed the Gardners a debt he would never be able to properly repay. Fact was, he owed them his life.

He smiled. He especially owed those two little towheads who'd found him lying beside the road. They quite literally saved his life.

He kept the bay in a handsome trot the whole half dozen miles out there and was delighted to see smoke coming from the chimney and the pair of mules picking at some sprigs of grass beside the corral fence line.

"Hello the house," he called as he came near.

Longarm was grinning ear to ear when he pulled the bay to a halt in the yard near the chicken coop. It felt practically like a homecoming to him.

Jean and the boys came tumbling out, and as soon as they recognized their visitor they too were smiling. Jean knelt and said, "Boys, run get your father. Tell him we're having company for dinner." Then she hurried the rest of the way to where Longarm stood and gave him a huge, welcoming hug.

She stepped back a pace and eyed him top to bottom, then her smile returned and she said, "You're looking well. You look fit." She laughed. "But I think you need a good feed. Would you mind killing a chicken while I go and set some bread? Roasted chicken this time, though, not just the broth that you must have gotten so tired of."

"Roasted chicken sounds fine, an' I brought a fruitcake for dessert if that'd be all right with you an' the boys. Slab o' beef too. Figured you might not get that real often, leastways as I recall. Brought a little o' this-an'-that for about everybody."

Jean's eyes lighted and she declared, "We'll have us a party, mister."

He laughed. "You're still calling me mister?"

"Will mister be all right? It won't offend?"

"Dear Jean, I don't think there's much of anything that you an' Tom could do that I would ever take offense to. Now, grab an armload o' this stuff and go tend to your bread-making. I'll fetch that chicken, if I ain't forgot how to handle one of them critters, and follow along with the rest o' this plunder. Go on now."

The woman was smiling when she turned back to

the house, and that did Longarm's heart good. Shortly after, Tom came rushing out of his mine with both lads skipping and jumping at his heels.

Yes, Longarm thought, it was definitely time that they all had themselves a party. And he was just the boy to handle one.

Chapter 45

Longarm pushed back from the table with a groan as he patted his belly and expressed his gratitude in that, the most genuine way possible. "Mighty fine, Jean. That was mighty fine. Now, if you good folks will excuse me, I'd best be getting back to town."

"Oh, can't you stay the night, Mister? Surely you can spare us just the one night."

The Gardners called him Mister—in a fond, almost familial way—and Longarm had resisted giving them a name. He did not want to lie to them by telling them he was Jim Stevens, but it would not do for anyone here to know his real name and job. It was bad enough that Belle knew him, but that had been unavoidable. So he and they alike settled on the friendly moniker of "Mister."

"I wish that I could, Jean, but I got an appointment in town this afternoon." He laughed. "I'm already late for it." Whatever time Ira Small took his break would be past by the time Longarm reached Jensenville now, but he intended to be in the alley behind the place when the post office closed at 5:30. "Business before pleasure, as everybody always says."

Longarm stood and reached for his hat.

"It's a stupid saying," Tom put in.

"Please, Mister, please?" the boys begged. He tousled their hair but did not relent.

"I really need to be going, but I can promise you one thing. No matter what, I ain't never gonna forget you fine folks. You saved my life. Easy thing to say, but you really did, and I thank you for it."

"I understand," Tom said, "but I regret the necessity." He smiled. "Regret that you have to leave, that is, not that we helped when you were in need. Will you come back, Mister?"

"If I can. I'd like to, I can promise you that much." He thanked Jean again and gave each of the boys a shiny dime. Tom walked out to the surrey with him.

"Is everything all right, Mister?" the miner asked, genuine concern in his voice.

"Aye, pretty much." Longarm glanced around before he approached the buggy. He did not think it likely that the two plug-uglies would jump him here. Not again. But believing that could present them with an opportunity to do what he did not expect.

The problem was that it is not possible to expect everything.

But a man could try.

"Thanks again, Tom." Longarm shook the lines, and the bay high-stepped away from the Gardner place.

Chapter 46

The sons of bitches struck a mile down the road toward Jensenville. One moment the bay was striding peacefully along. The next, there was the high-pitched whine of a bullet zipping past Longarm's ears and the sound of it smacking into the roadside brush immediately thereafter.

The booming sound of the gunshot came from one direction. Longarm bailed out of the seat in the other direction.

He hit the ground hard, rolled over, and scrambled on hands and knees into a clump of scrub oak beside the road, Colt in hand but with no target to shoot at.

The bay horse laid its ears back, hiked its tail high, and bolted into a run, dragging the now empty surrey with it as it headed for town and barn and safety.

Longarm burrowed deeper into the tangled maze of gnarled branches and dry, crackling fallen leafs.

He heard another bullet reach the oaks, but the sound came from a good dozen yards away. Again the sound of the bullet was followed almost immediately by the report. The ambushers were not too distant then, he realized.

There would be two of them, he was sure. Neither of Mendenhall's bullyboys would have had the guts to come after him alone. So both would be somewhere in the rocks to the left of the road. Probably both had bolstered their courage with whiskey.

He doubted whether Marshal Jonathan Mendenhall would have come himself. Which meant it would be Wilson and Albrecht up there.

Longarm chided himself for not looking to see exactly where the gunsmoke from that first shot came from. It would have been useful to know precisely where they were hiding.

As it happened, though, he had been going in the other direction at the time. It had seemed sensible then, never mind that he regretted it now.

Another blindly probing bullet crackled through the tough scrub oak branches and slammed into the hard, rocky soil underneath the low spread of foliage. That one too hit yards away from Longarm.

If the bastards kept shooting, they just might possibly connect. After all, even a blind hog finds an acorn now and then.

And there were aplenty of acorns in this patch of oaks.

Longarm frowned in thought. Then began squirming and wriggling his way through the dead leaves back toward the road.

Wilson and Albrecht would surely expect him to go in the other direction so as to get away.

So he would do what he *hoped* they did not expect.

Chapter 47

Before he could get back to the edge of the oak patch, he heard two more shots fired álmost simultaneously and then quickly after them the sound of hoofbeats as at least one horse was booted into a hard run.

A ruse? he asked himself. Both Wilson and Albrecht might have fired together, then one of them jumped on a horse and hightailed it for the safety of town. The other could be lying in wait now, hoping Longarm would take that bait and show himself on the road, thinking both had given up their ambush.

The ambush site had to be sixty or seventy yards on the far side of the road, he judged. That would be duck soup for a man with a rifle but long range for a revolver.

Longarm thought it over and decided he was not in a gambling mood this afternoon.

Maybe there was a rifleman over there. Maybe

there was nothing but a handful of expended cartridge cases.

The thing was, no purpose would be served by exposing himself to the far hillside, and much peace of mind would be gained from staying where he was, hidden and safe within the scrub oaks.

Custis Long had patience, especially when it came to keeping his skin free of bullets.

He quietly cleared a space for himself among the dry leaves and bits of broken scrub. Then, .45 still in hand, he placed his hat on the ground and used it for a pillow while he made himself comfortable right where he was.

He was content now to wait for sundown. Just in case.

Chapter 48

Jensenville, Colorado, was not Longarm's favorite town. Not by a long shot it was not. But its lights were awfully welcome when the town came in sight at the far end of the gulch where it was found.

Longarm stopped at the livery before heading on into town. He walked toward the back of the barn and peered over the boards into the stall where the bay was kept. The animal was standing there, its nose in a feed bunk.

"That's the second time a horse you rented came back on its own," the hostler said from behind him.

Longarm turned to face the man.

"Don't you come back here and try to rent another. Not never," the fellow spat. "You aren't welcome. You hear me?"

Longarm nodded. "I heard you. Don't blame you neither."

"Damn horse was all lathered up and about wore out. I had to walk him for better than a half hour just to bring him down."

Longarm dug into his pockets and found a five-dollar half eagle. He handed it to the hostler. "For your time," he said.

The man grunted, scowling. But he took the coin and tucked it into a pocket. "Don't come back," he said, turning away.

Longarm walked out into the street and made his way up to Belle's saloon. He was dried out after the hours spent inside that patch of scrub oaks and the subsequent walk back to town. He was hungry too, but first he wanted something to drink.

Then perhaps he would go hunting.

Belle was standing behind the bar, speaking with her bartender Andy when Longarm entered.

"You look tired, Jim," she said. "You're all sweaty. And what is that stuff stuck on your coat? Twigs?" She came to him and began brushing the bits of oak trash off him. "What can I do for you?"

"A shot an' a beer would be nice," he told her, "an' some o' what you got on that free lunch platter."

Belle smiled. "I think I can do better than that, Jim. Why don't you go on back to my office. I'll be along in just a few minutes."

Longarm nodded and headed for the office that he remembered so very well from previous visits. The sofa was an especially pleasant memory. But right now he was not in the mood for such.

He sat on the sofa. Belle joined him only a few

minutes later carrying a heavy tray laden with two beers, two glasses of rye whiskey, and a plate with an assortment of eggs, pickles, and ham.

She set the tray down on her desk, picked up a beer and a glass, and handed those to him before going back for the plate of food. She sat on the couch beside him.

Longarm helped himself to everything in sight, then said, "Aren't you joining me?"

Belle shook her head. "I've already had my supper, and I don't want anything to drink right now. Those are for you, Custis."

He leaned over and kissed her left temple. "You're a marvel, girl. Thanks."

"What else can I do for you?" she asked.

"D'you know where Mendenhall an' his bullyboys hang out?"

"Chuck and Cory, do you mean? They like to drink at the Hardrock."

He raised an eyebrow.

"The Hardrock is the third building up, other side of the street," Belle said.

"Should they be there at this hour?" he asked.

"Probably. They like to play cards there, them and a handful of cronies."

"And Mendenhall himself?"

"He is probably at home with his wife."

"A piece o' shit like him is married?" Longarm mused. "Kinda makes one wonder about how blind women can be, doesn't it?"

"Do you want me to get him? I can bring him here

if you like. I could send a message that I'm having trouble with some customers. That would bring him."

Longarm shook his head. "No, thanks. I expect I can get him out when I want him."

Gunfire should do the trick, he was thinking. And he did expect there would be some of that happening in Jensenville very soon.

He finished his beer and stood. He bent down and gave Belle a gentle kiss on the lips. "You are a good girl, Miz Coyne. Don't let nobody ever tell you different."

Then he turned and headed for the Hardrock. Three doors up and on the far side of the street.

Chuck Wilson and Cory Albrecht would likely be there drinking and playing cards.

He wondered if they would be willing to play with him now, face-to-face instead of from ambush.

Chapter 49

The Hardrock was about as much a casino as it was a saloon. There was a short bar near the front. The remainder of the large room was devoted to gaming tables of various sorts, some dealing poker and some monte. There was a wheel of fortune—too easy to rig, Longarm always thought—plus roulette.

The place was fairly crowded, mostly with men wearing the rough, mud-stained clothing of miners, plus two barkeeps and what looked like a pit boss. Longarm wondered if this was another of Belle's establishments. He should have asked when he had the chance.

The smells of cigar smoke, stale beer, and sawdust greeted him when he came in. Those scents had a pleasant, homey attraction for him. He found them pretty much everywhere he went, and he liked them.

At the back of the big room were three women wearing very modest, throat-to-floor, long-sleeved dresses. Or so they appeared until they turned to face in the other direction. There was no back to the dresses, just thin strings at neck and waist to hold them together. Their asses and backs were completely naked.

It was an interesting touch, Longarm thought. Maybe more than interesting. Two of the girls had very nice shapes. The third was a little chunky. But not too terribly bad, he judged. A man could find worse. Hell, he himself had fucked worse. And more than once too.

His interest at the moment, however, was not in women. It was in trouble.

He found it sitting at a card table toward the back of the smoky room.

Cory Albrecht was in the process of dealing cards to four other men at his table. His concentration was fixed on the deck of pasteboards in his hand, so he did not see Longarm enter the room.

Longarm made his way through the crowd, winding back and forth among the tables, until he was within a few paces of Albrecht's table.

The big deputy looked up, casually looking around the room before he took a look at the cards he had dealt himself.

He saw Longarm and went suddenly pale, all color draining from his face but his neck becoming flushed dark red.

"You . . . uh . . . Shit!"

Albrecht dropped the cards in his hand and grabbed for the pistol at his waist.

Longarm waited until the local deputy had his

revolver in hand before Longarm reached for his own .45.

It was no contest. Longarm drew and fired in a flash. A 250-grain lead slug pierced Albrecht's forehead. The back of his skull was blown out and about two cupfuls of gray-and-red gore splattered the wall behind him.

Albrecht rocked backward in his chair, then slumped forward onto the green baize of the card table.

The man who had been sitting at Albrecht's right side leaped to his feet, took a look at what was left of the back of the deputy's skull, and began to puke all over the card table.

Another who had been playing at that table jumped up and started to pull his pistol. A look at Longarm's eyes changed his mind. He took his hand away from the butt of his revolver and sat primly down in his chair, hands folded on top of the table in plain sight.

"Wilson," Longarm snapped. "Where is he?"

No one at the table spoke.

But the man who was just finishing depositing his supper onto the card table gave a fearful glance toward the back of the big room. Where the whores were.

Longarm took a step backward, .45 still in his hand, and looked toward a door leading somewhere in the rear.

The smoke in the barroom had the sharp scent of burned gunpowder in it now, and there was a stampede toward the batwings at the front.

The bartender reached underneath his bar.

"Don't," Longarm snapped.

The barkeep brought his hands out to the bar surface. He picked up a bar rag and pretended to polish the rough, beer-soaked surface in front of him.

Wilson had to be back there, Longarm thought.

And Chuck Wilson was by far the more dangerous of the pair of thugs.

Chapter 50

A hand, an eyeball, and the gaping muzzle of a .45 revolver appeared close beside the doorjamb of that back door.

Longarm ducked. The pistol by the door bellowed, and behind him the back-bar mirror shattered, shards of broken glass cascading to the floor.

Longarm snapped a shot, firing not directly at the place where the pistol had been quickly withdrawn, but at the wall beside that spot, hoping his bullet would penetrate the wall and find flesh behind it.

There was no answering yelp of pain, or any sound of a body falling to the floor.

He stood. Moved swiftly to his right, and hunkered down behind an overturned table.

The place had cleared out now. Even the bartenders had fled, leaving Longarm alone in the saloon.

Longarm flicked the loading gate of his Colt open and quickly punched out his empty cartridge cases, replacing them with fresh rounds. He closed the loading gate and shifted back to his left so he could get a better look at the doorway.

Wilson's revolver showed again. Briefly. Only long enough to throw another shot in Longarm's general direction. The bullet flew harmlessly overhead and thudded into the front wall of the Hardrock.

Immediately afterward there was the sound of running feet and the slam of a door.

A ruse? It could have been.

It could also mean that Wilson was on the run, trying to get away from retribution.

Longarm chose to believe that the man was running. He took the chance and charged toward the back of the saloon. Charged into and through the doorway. Into a hall with cribs on either side where the girls could ply their fleshy trade.

A whore in a yellow dress stood in one of the doorways. She would be the reason Wilson had not been out front with his buddy Albrecht, Longarm guessed.

He did not bother to ask her where Wilson had gone. There was a back door and that surely had to be the answer to that unspoken question.

Longarm ran through the short hallway but stopped at the back door.

Wilson could very likely be in the alley beyond, lying in wait, pistol ready.

Longarm took a deep breath.

And yanked the door open.

Chapter 51

There was . . . nothing. No gunshot. No pounding feet. No shouts or threats or anger. Longarm found himself alone in the discarded litter of the alley that ran between the Hardrock Saloon and the creek where the Jensenville gold strike was originally found.

Longarm stood there hunched over with tension, his nerves on edge. He had been beaten up and shot at just about enough since he came here. He wanted to get some back at the sons of bitches who were doing such things, but right now he had no one to shoot at and it annoyed him.

He shoved his .45 back into its leather and straightened up, shuddering and squaring his shoulders. He took a deep breath and was deliberately slow to let it out.

Then he turned and went back into the Hardrock.

One of the two barkeeps and the natty fellow who seemed to be the casino pit boss or to play some such role were standing beside Albrecht's cooling corpse. They eyed Longarm nervously when he entered the saloon. There was no sign of anyone else, including the whore in the yellow dress.

"You, uh . . ." The pit boss stammered wordlessly for a moment, then shut up.

"You," Longarm said, nodding toward the bartender. "Give me a rye. Don't bother with a chaser."

"Y-yessir." The man practically scuttled around behind his bar. His hand shook when he poured the rye, and he spilled a little on the bar. He filled a water glass to the brim and spilled a little more carrying it out from behind the bar.

The man did not ask to be paid for the drink and Longarm did not offer.

Cory Albrecht's body had not been moved, but Longarm noticed that someone had confiscated the small pile of money that had been in front of his place at the table.

"Did somebody call for the barber?" Longarm asked.

"I sent a man for him," the pit boss or manager or whatever he was—Belle's employee more than likely—responded.

"And the town marshal?"

The fellow nodded. "Him too."

Longarm grunted softly to himself. That was just fine. It was going to come down to a face-off between him and Mendenhall eventually anyway. Now would be just as good as later.

"You boys might want to clear out before there's more lead flying," he advised.

The bartender and manager took his advice and got the hell out of the place while they still could.

With a sigh, Longarm carried his tumbler of rye whiskey—a taste told him that while it might indeed be rye, it was not a very good rye, cheap stuff—over to a table close to Cory Albrecht's body.

"Now let's see how good your pals are, Cory," he told the dead man. "Let's see which of us joins you six feet down."

He took another very small sip of the very poor rye whiskey. And waited.

Chapter 52

He did not have long to wait. Within ten minutes or less he heard footsteps beyond the batwings. They stopped just short of the doorway.

"Stevens. Come out of there, Stevens. You're under arrest." It sounded like Mendenhall. Longarm guessed that Wilson would be backing him up.

Longarm sat with his legs crossed, .45 held in his lap. He took a sip of rye before he answered. "I think we can work this out, Marshal. What I done was pure self-defense. Your man drew on me."

"That isn't the way I heard it," the voice came back.

"That's the way I'm telling it, an' I got a hundred reasons why it's the truth."

"A hundred?" the voice asked.

"You heard me right, Marshal, an' my alibi is golden."

"In gold, you say."

"On the barrelhead," Longarm answered.

"Maybe I didn't hear it right the first time," Mendenhall called from the doorway. "Maybe this was self-defense after all."

"You have the word of my witnesses on it," Longarm said.

"I'm coming in," the marshal said. "No guns. Just me."

"What about your deputy?" Longarm responded. "I don't trust him. Him an' Albrecht was buddies."

"What I say goes in this town," Mendenhall said, still prudently staying out of sight.

"Have your man drop his gunbelt an' come in with you," Longarm instructed. "You can keep your gun but not in your hand."

"All right. That sounds fair. Just give me your word that you won't shoot. That is good enough for me."

"My word," Longarm said, his lips pulled back into something that resembled a smile. "An' my witnesses."

"Right. We, uh, we're coming in now."

There was a moment's pause, then Mendenhall showed himself behind the batwings. He pushed them open and stepped into the Hardrock, hands held well away from the revolver in his holster.

Longarm nodded. "Now your man."

Mendenhall turned his head and said something, then Chuck Wilson moved into sight. He was not wearing a gunbelt.

"Turn around," Longarm said.

Wilson looked puzzled. "Why?"

"'Cause you could have your pistol stuffed into your britches at the small o' your back." It was what Longarm would have done if their positions had been reversed. Besides, he did not like Wilson and wanted to make him eat a little shit.

"Go to hell," Wilson snapped.

"Do it, Chuck," Mendenhall ordered.

Reluctantly, Wilson turned.

Longarm grinned. The man did indeed have a revolver in his waistband at his back. "Lay it on the floor. Nice an' easy."

Wilson very carefully took the pistol out, bent, and placed it on the sawdust at his feet. He said something under his breath. Longarm did not mind. He would have been pissed off too had he been in Wilson's place.

"Now, you boys come an' set down. We'll share a drink an' talk about the good times."

"First we need to talk about your witnesses," Mendenhall said.

"Right." Colt still in his right hand, Longarm dipped two fingers of his left hand into his vest pocket and came out with a gold coin. Then another. And another, until he had five of the twenty-dollar double eagles lying on the table in front of him.

"Solid gold witnesses," he said.

"Impeccable," Mendenhall agreed. "Chuck, go behind the bar over there and get us something to drink. We'll want to toast this new partnership with Mr. Stevens."

"Yes, sir."

"Can we get you something?" Mendenhall asked.

Longarm motioned toward his nearly full glass of rye. "I'm good, thanks."

"Just the two then, Chuck."

"Yes, sir."

Longarm kept an eye on the man, aware that the barkeep more than likely had a pistol or perhaps a sawed-off shotgun underneath that bar, but all Wilson did was pick up glasses, fill them, and return.

"Sit, gentlemen. Make yourselves comfortable," Longarm said.

Mendenhall smiled and picked up the five pieces of gold. They quickly disappeared into his pocket. Then he and Wilson both raised their glasses toward Longarm, Mendenhall smiling but Wilson looking like he was having a tooth yanked out of his face.

"To your good health, Mr. Stevens," Mendenhall said. "Good health and a long life."

"And to yours," Longarm said in return, taking a sip of the truly awful rye whiskey.

Chapter 53

"Now," Longarm said when they each had taken a drink, "tell me about this partnership of ours."

"It's simple," Mendenhall said. He reached into his pocket for a cotton pouch of tobacco and rolled himself a cigarette. When he was finished with the quirly, Wilson struck a match and leaned forward to light the smoke for the marshal. "Whatever fiddles you got going here. With Boss. With that asshole Ira Small. With Belle Coyne. With any-damn-body, Stevens. Whatever game you're into, I get ten percent."

"That's interestin'," Longarm said. "Boss takes half."

"Boss takes whatever I allow him to get." The man tipped his head back and blew a smoke ring then laughed. "He also gets to call himself Boss. Which he isn't." Mendenhall's expression hardened and he leaned forward in his chair. "Understand this. I run

this town. And I get a piece of whatever you drag in.
Are we clear about this, Stevens?"

"Perfectly clear," Longarm's lips thinned into
what passed for a smile, "boss."

"Good. Excellent. Chucky, go get your gun and
belt. You look naked sitting there without them."

Wilson obediently rose and went to do what the
marshal said. Longarm lifted an eyebrow.

"He won't bother you," Mendenhall said.

Longarm nodded. "Your word is good enough for
me." He paused then said, "And if Chucky wants to
go off the reservation," he looked at Cory Albrecht,
whose brains were still decorating the wall in the
Hardrock, "he'll get a taste o' this. But no hard feel-
in's between you an' me if he does."

"Fair enough," Mendenhall said.

Longarm took a drink of whiskey and lighted a
cheroot, then said, "Mind if I ask you something?"

"Go ahead."

"Boss Carter. What's his fiddle?"

"Money, of course. From his mines and from most
things in town. Of course everything funnels through
me, which is how I get mine. And from the men who
work the mines." Mendenhall laughed. "He keeps
the poor bastards as slaves."

"That is, uh . . ."

"Yeah, I know. Slavery is illegal these days, but it
hasn't disappeared. Just changed somewhat. What
Carter does is to offer good pay, but he charges them
for their bunks, their food, their tools. He charges
them more than they could possibly earn. And if a
man wants to leave without paying off his debt to us,

why, me and my boys go after him and, um, teach him not to be doing any such of a thing."

"Like they taught me out on the road?" Longarm asked.

Mendenhall nodded. "Like that. Except I will admit, Chucky here and the late Mr. Albrecht took a dislike to you for some reason. They carried things a little too far."

"A little far," Longarm said, rubbing the back of his head with his left hand. The right was still occupied with holding the revolver in his lap. "Is it the same with that Negro pet of his?"

"Delilah? Oh, yes. She got the idea that she wanted to leave. She doesn't think that now."

"So Carter has all those slaves making money for him," Longarm said.

Mendenhall laughed. "Making it for me."

"And Coyne?"

"Like them all, she pays, but she pays through me. As far as she knows she's paying her dues to Carter."

"And me?" Longarm asked.

"Just pay your ten percent. We won't have any more troubles between us."

Longarm took a drag on his cheroot then tossed back the last of the rye. "I'm glad we had this little talk." He meant it too. Now all he had to do was to finish his business with Ira Small and wrap things up here. It likely would take a whole herd of Justice Department lawyers to figure out all the charges to be filed.

Something else occurred to him, and he asked, "My deal with Small. How'd you know about that?"

"I had a good deal going with Grady Handleman until you went and killed him. It was obvious you were stepping in where Handleman left off." Mendenhall dropped his cigarette butt to the floor and ground it out under his boot. "Come to think of it, this is two of my people you've had to shoot." He grinned. "In self-defense, of course. The thing is, if this keeps up, I could run out of people to make money for me."

More than you could possibly know, Longarm thought. Once his badge came out into the open, Jonathan Mendenhall's scam would be bringing in a whole lot less. Like . . . nothing at all.

"What about Generest?" he asked. If the postmaster was in on any of this, he would have to be included in the general roundup.

"Aw, he knows nothing about any of it. The man acts like a damn saint or something. I think if he ever found out about Small, he would fire the man or turn him over to the federals or something. To tell you the truth, I would have gotten rid of him, but we don't get to pick who our postmaster is. That's assigned by somebody down in Denver. Anyway I get my little bit through Small, so I don't worry about Generest so much. Why? Does it matter?"

Longarm shook his head. "Not to me, it don't. I was just curious, that's all."

Mendenhall finished his drink and stood. "It's been good talking with you, Stevens. I don't think we'll have any more trouble. Just pay my ten percent." He laughed. "And whatever you owe Carter, you pay that through me too."

Longarm nodded. "Good enough," he said.

Partners. Sure they were.

But he waited until the marshal and his deputy were out of the saloon before he returned his .45 to the leather.

Chapter 54

"Hey, you!" the bartender barked at Longarm as people slowly began to filter back into the Hardrock Saloon.

Longarm stopped. Turned. Looked at the man.

"Clean up your mess." The fellow pointed to the corpse that was still slumped onto the otherwise empty poker table.

"Oh, the marshal is gonna take care o' that," Longarm lied. He continued on his way out of the saloon and onto the street.

The mountain air was clean and brisk, and Longarm felt good. He walked over to the post office and went in, but there was no sign of Ira Small. The postmaster, Herb Generest, was behind the counter. Longarm pretended interest in the few Wanted posters pinned to a corkboard on the wall, then wandered out again.

It was good to know that Generest was an honest man. Longarm had been beginning to think there was no such thing in Jensenville.

He walked down to Belle's headquarters saloon. Andy was behind the bar, and there were a handful of customers scattered through the place.

"Is the lady here?" Longarm asked.

Andy shook his head. "Not right now. She didn't say where she was going, but I understand there was some trouble at another of her places. She might've gone up there."

Belle had not gone to the Hardrock. Longarm was sure of that. Of course she might have had to go somewhere else in connection with the events over here. Like maybe arranging for someone to carry Albrecht over to the barber for embalming. And for someone to scrub down the floor and the wall. That needed doing too.

It seemed a damn shame that she was not present, though. Longarm was kind of horny, and a little time spent with Belle Coyne would not have been a bad thing.

Another time, he thought.

"Anything I can do for you, Mr. Stevens?"

"Some of the good rye would be nice," Longarm said. That would help get the taste of the cheap stuff out of his mouth. "And a beer to chase it with. Maybe some of those cheroots I see over there."

"Whatever you want, Mr. Stevens."

Longarm spent a few minutes with his drinks, then used his teeth to nip the twist off the end of one

of the cheroots. He lighted the slender cigar with a
match Andy offered, then nodded. "I'm goin' over to
the hotel. If Ira Small comes in, please tell him that's
where I've gone, would you?"

"I'll see to it myself," Andy promised.

Longarm turned and went back outside.

Chapter 55

ngarm woke with a start. He must have dozed off, cause the room was dark and there was no hint of ylight outside his hotel room window. He sat up the side of the bed and struck a match. He lifted globe of the bedside lamp and touched his match the wick then carefully adjusted the flame to a nice tterfly shape.

He stood and stretched. Reached for the coat he d laid beside him on the bed and pulled it on.

Small had not showed up, dammit. He would have go looking for the man. Later. First he wanted to d something to eat, something to shut up the rum-ng in his belly.

Out of habit he touched the grips of his .45 to sure himself that the revolver was where it should . Then he rubbed a hand over his hair, smoothed mustache, and gave the ends a twist. He reached his hat and put that on, then went out.

Willard was on duty behind the desk. Longarm gave the man a friendly nod and continued on o into the street.

Street lamps glowed up and down Jensenville main street, and there were sounds of merrime coming from the saloons. Across the creek th whorehouse was practically aflame with lamps, ma of them red so there could be no doubt as to the bus ness that was conducted there.

Thinking about that was enough to give Longar a hard-on, and he gave some thought to walking t the street to Boss Carter's place. It would be mo than pleasant if he could pry Delilah loose for a litt while and bring her back to his room.

The pretty black girl could suck a dick so hard would clean a man's toenails. From the inside.

Smiling at the thought of her, he continued up th street to the café.

"The usual, Mr. Stevens?" he was greeted with

Longarm nodded. "The usual, Thomas." H stopped at the counter long enough to collect a cu of coffee and a copy of the *Rocky Mountain News*– only three days old, not bad—and continued on t the table in the far corner of the place. He liked hav ing his back to a wall, a habit that had saved his li on more than one occasion.

His supper of steak, biscuits, and loads of grav was delivered in short order.

Longarm was halfway through his meal whe trouble came calling.

Chapter 56

"You son of a bitch!"

Chuck Wilson was drunk as a lord, staggering from side to side and barely able to remain upright. He almost fell. He grabbed the back of a chair for support and instead got a handful of the hair of the lady who happened to be occupying that chair.

The woman shrieked and tried to pull away. Wilson unfortunately kept his grip on her. When she moved, it pulled the drunken Wilson off balance. He fell forward, landing on the woman's back.

The two of them tumbled to the floor. The gentleman who was dining with the lady, presumably her husband, jumped into action, yanking Wilson off the woman and pulling at his companion in an effort to get her onto her feet.

Wilson apparently took exception to being handled like that. He snarled and wobbled upright.

"Bastard," Wilson shouted. Longarm was not

entirely clear if Wilson was calling the gentleman diner that or if he was merely complaining to the world in general. Whatever his meaning, the focus of his whiskey-addled fury shifted from Longarm to the man whose wife he had grabbed.

Chuck Wilson hauled his revolver out and waved it in the direction of the man, who by now had his wife back in her chair and was himself standing almost belly to belly with Wilson.

As far as Longarm could see, the gentleman whose dinner had been so rudely interrupted was not himself armed.

That seemed to make no difference to Chuck Wilson, if indeed Wilson noticed that the fellow had no weapon with which to defend himself.

"You can't . . . throw me . . . round so easy," Wilson growled between hiccups. "Matter of . . . honor."

Honor? Deputy Wilson, the man who collected dirty money and broke heads for a living? Really? Longarm was astonished.

He was appalled, however, when Wilson pulled the trigger.

The small café was filled with the roar of the gunshot and the stink of burned gunpowder.

There were a dozen or so people having their dinners at the time. Nearly all of them ducked for the floor.

All except Custis Long and the gentleman whose wife Wilson had manhandled. Long because he was bringing his own revolver into play. The gentleman diner because he was standing upright, staring down at a bright red stain that had appeared on his belly.

a stain that was quickly spreading as blood flowed from a fresh wound.

"Ha!" Wilson barked. "That'll show you, sumbish."

Wilson wobbled, nearly fell down, and once again grabbed for a chair to offer support. This time he succeeded in taking hold of the chair. He belched, swayed front to back, and belched again.

The man fixed his eyes once more on Longarm and scowled. "You," he shouted. "Bastard." Which at least cleared up his meaning when he'd shouted the same word earlier.

The gent Wilson had just shot fell, his knees buckling. His wife screamed, and he fell on top of her, as if shielding her from the gunfire. And that could indeed have been his intent, Longarm thought.

By then Longarm's Colt was in his hand and aimed at Deputy Chuck Wilson.

"Drop the gun, Wilson. What you done here is murder, and I'll see you hang for it."

"Huh? What? Who the fuck? Oh. You." Wilson carefully, and with the intense deliberation that a drunk will apply to even the smallest task, reached up with his free hand to pull the hammer of his revolver back for another shot. "Gonna kill your ass. Kill your ass."

"Don't," Longarm warned.

Wilson ignored him and shifted his concentration from the pistol to Longarm.

"Shit," Longarm mumbled.

And shot the idiot son of a bitch in the center of his chest.

Chapter 57

The town barber was called—the man must have been making a fortune from his undertaking sideline ever since Longarm came to town—to clear away the bodies, both of Wilson and the poor chap Wilson had murdered.

The newly widowed wife was in hysterics. Longarm suspected that if Wilson had not already been dead, the lady would have killed the son of a bitch herself. As it was there was nothing he could do for her, so he got the hell out of there before she thought to turn her fury in his direction for being the cause of it all. Which was not the way he viewed things, but he could see how she might come to that conclusion.

Instead he headed down to Belle's for a spot of whiskey and to look for Ira Small. There was no sign of the little postal clerk, so Longarm settled for the whiskey and a stroll back to his hotel.

Town marshal Jonathan Mendenhall was there in
the lobby waiting for him, along with another man
Longarm had not seen before. Mendenhall's sidekick
was wearing a badge pinned to his vest and had a
double-barrel shotgun in his hands.

"We had an agreement," Mendenhall snapped as
soon as Longarm entered the lobby. "We were all
going to get along. But you couldn't stand by it. You
just had to go ahead and murder my man Wilson."

Longarm blinked. "Murder? That ain't exactly the
way I seen it. Ask anybody who was dining there.
Wilson came in gunning for me, drunk as a lord an'
feeling mean. He's the one as done murder. Murdered
that poor man that done nothing wrong but to take
his lady out to dinner. All I done was to enforce
the law."

"Enforce the law my ass!" Mendenhall snarled. "I
said we could get along. I never said anything about
making you a deputy. You had no authority to enforce
anything, and I'm taking you in on the charge of
murder in the first degree. Now, hand over that
shooter and put your wrists out so I can cuff you."

"I don't think so," Longarm said. He sighed. "I
wasn't ready to do this quite yet, but you're forcing
me here, Marshal, so I reckon I'm the one has to place
you under arrest."

"You have no authority, Stevens. You . . ."

"I have all the authority I need, mister. I'm a deputy United States marshal, and the name ain't Stevens, it's Long. Custis Long."

Mendenhall blanched a pale white, leading Longarm to suspect that his name was not unknown here.

"Are you coming quiet?" Longarm asked.

His attention was more on the deputy than on Mendenhall, which was a good thing as the man decided to do his boss a favor by gunning down a U.S. marshal.

It was a mistake. Before he could bring his scattergun to bear and yank the hammers back, Longarm had his Colt out.

Flame, smoke, and hot lead burst from the barrel of the .45. The slug hit the hapless deputy on the breastbone just below his throat. It ripped out his windpipe and severed his spine before bursting out the back of his neck.

The man dropped like a marionette with its strings cut. The shotgun fell harmlessly to the floor.

Mendenhall was left flat-footed, his pistol still in the leather. "I . . . I give up. Don't shoot me. For God's sake, man, don't shoot me." The marshal threw his empty hands high.

Longarm grunted. He kept his .45 trained on the marshal's belly and said, "Turn around. Keep your hands where they are."

Mendenhall complied without complaint and held his hands in the air while Longarm snagged the marshal's revolver out of its holster and took the man's handcuffs off his belt.

"One hand at a time now. Bring 'em down to the small o' your back."

Once Mendenhall was safely handcuffed, Longarm marched him over and into a cell at the town jail, where a bleary-eyed drunk tried and failed to figure out what was going on in the adjoining cell

Unable to work it out, the drunk rolled over to face the other way and was soon snoring.

Longarm securely locked Mendenhall into the cell and started to hang the cell key on the wall peg where he had found it. Then it occurred to him that some acquaintance or crony of the corrupt marshal could come along and release him. Longarm slipped the key into his coat pocket instead.

"I'll be back," he told the unhappy marshal. Then he grinned. "Or not."

There were two more things he needed to do before the seemingly simple crime of theft of postage could be wrapped up and turned over to the United States attorney for prosecution. And in Mendenhall's case, the crime would be turned over to Colorado state authorities, unless he could figure out a federal angle to the man's thefts and assaults and malfeasance in office.

Bastard! Longarm thought as he returned to the hotel so he could retrieve his wallet and badge from the false bottom on his Gladstone bag. He turned the wallet out so the badge was exposed and hung it in the breast pocket of his coat, on prominent display there.

Chapter 58

A handful of inquiries brought Longarm to a small
and rather shabby house on the poor side of the
creek that ran through Jensenville. He mounted the
stoop and rapped on the screen door. The inside
door was opened several moments later. Longarm
was confronted by a very large woman, almost as
fat as Boss Carter. And with a sparse, dark mustache
on her upper lip. She was a formidable beast, he
thought.

Still, she was a woman and presumed to be a lady.
He snatched his hat off. "Ma'am," he said in greeting. "I'm looking for Ira Small. I was told he lives
here. Is that correct?"

"I am Mrs. Small. Anything you have to say to Ira
can be said to me."

"I, uh, I don't think so," Longarm said. "Not this
time."

"I shall take a message if there is one. Otherwise I must ask you to leave."

"Well, I can't do that, Miz Small. Y'see, I'm a deputy U.S. marshal. Custis Long is my name. And I'm here to arrest your husband."

"Arrest him! What has that sniveling little weasel done this time?"

"He's been stealing from the post office, ma'am, and that's a federal offense. I got to take him down to Denver and put him in jail there until he's arraigned and stands trial. Now, please, ma'am, I need to see your husband. Is he here?"

For a moment Longarm thought the woman was going to argue with him. She hesitated but eventually moved aside and opened the screen door for him to enter.

"Ira is in the parlor." She pointed the way.

When Longarm stepped into the tiny room, Small was seated in a cushioned armchair reading a recent *Denver Post*. When he saw Longarm, he stood and the beginnings of a welcoming smile touched the corners of his lips.

Then he saw the badge Longarm was displaying and the welcome crumpled.

"You . . . aren't . . ."

"I'm not James Stevens, Mr. Small. My name is Long."

"The one they call Longarm?"

Longarm nodded. "The same."

Oddly, Small did smile then. "It was good while it lasted," he said and held his wrists out for Longarm to apply handcuffs.

Longarm secured the bracelets on Small's thin wrists, tipped his Stetson to Mrs. Small, and led Small outside and to the jail.

"You'll stay in here overnight, Ira, then down to Denver. It won't be too awful bad on you, I hope. I'll put a word in with your jailers so they don't put you in with the sort that'd rape you."

"Rape? But I'm a man."

"Trust me, Ira. I know more about jails than I reckon you do. But I'll ask them to be easy with you."

"I never thought about, uh, that sort of thing. I thought about being caught, of course." He smiled again. "But it was worth it."

"Worth it? Really?"

Small nodded. "Oh, yes. You see, my wife handles all of our money. I wanted some of my own so I could step out with Miss Belle's fancy women." The little man's eyes went wide. "Why, do you know it? Those girls will actually suck a man's peter if you want them to."

Longarm could just guess what the poor son of a bitch had been getting at home. Hell, with that to come home to, Longarm probably would have risked federal prison too.

"I expect now, Ira, you'll get a chance to see how that is from the other side o' things."

"Whatever do you mean?"

"You'll see. But for now I'll try an' have them go easy with you. Come on in now. I got to put you in the cell here."

Longarm turned the drunk loose and locked Small

to that cell. Mendenhall was glaring bullets at him ut said nothing.

The only remaining thing to be done, Longarm ought, was to confront Boss Carter. Then perhaps e could go back to his hotel room and get some eep.

Chapter 59

"It's late," the bodyguard at the door said. "Boss asleep."

"Bullshit," Longarm responded. "I seen the ligh on in his room." That was easy enough. The palatia room occupied half the downstairs floor of the buil ing, maybe more than half. "By the way, if anybod wanted to kill your boss, all he'd have to do woul be to shoot through the window. It'd be easy."

"For God's sake, don't tell him that," the bodyguar said. "He'd have us standing outside his damn wi dows summer or winter, all day and all night too."

Longarm laughed. And entered the inner sanctu uninvited. The bodyguard had taken one look at th badge prominently displayed at Longarm's brea pocket and offered no objection.

"Mr. Stevens," Carter said from his familiar spo behind the big desk, despite the late hour, Delila

anding behind him. "What brings me the pleasure
'your . . . Oh." Longarm guessed that Boss too had
otted the badge. "You are . . .?"

"Deputy United States marshal outa the Denver
fice. And the name is Long, not Stevens."

"As in Longarm?"

"You've heard of me then."

"Nothing good, I assure you."

"In that case," Longarm said, "you probably heard
ght."

For a moment Longarm thought the big man was
ing to make a play for a gun. He did not. He tensed,
it after a moment he relaxed his posture and placed
oth hands on top of his desk. "Have you come to
rest me?" Carter asked.

Longarm shook his head. "No. The way I under-
and it, your kinda slavery is a matter o' money, not
ains. What I will do is talk to the U.S. attorney
hen I get back down to Denver. If he says he can
osecute, I'll come back up for you. I know where
can find you. With all you got invested here and all
u're bringing in from it, I know you ain't gonna go
where." He smiled. "For now all I intend is to do
take Delilah with me for company on my way
ack."

"But she . . ."

"Don't belong to you, is what she does, Carter.
ou know that. I know that. I'll make sure she knows
. And I know I can find a place for her down there.
Vhatever she has to do, it will be better than bein'
ur girl up here."

"You bastard," Carter said.

Longarm laughed. "I couldn't begin to tell yo how many times I been called that."

He held his hand out and Delilah came to him.

Watch for

LONGARM AND SEÑORITA REVENGE

the 415th novel in the exciting LONGARM
series from Jove

Coming in June!

LONGARM

GIANT-SIZED ADVENTURE FROM
AVENGING ANGEL LONGARM.

BY TABOR EVANS

penguin.com/actionwesterns